# Father To My Siblings

# Father To My Siblings

Olivier Sempiga

PARTRIDGE

Because of the dynamic nature of the Internet, any web addresses or links contained in this book may have changed since publication and may no longer be valid. The views expressed in this work are solely those of the author and do not necessarily reflect the views of the publisher, and the publisher hereby disclaims any responsibility for them.

Print information available on the last page.

**To order additional copies of this book, contact**
Toll Free 0800 990 914 (South Africa)
+44 20 3014 3997 (outside South Africa)
orders.africa@partridgepublishing.com

www.partridgepublishing.com/africa

"This is a must read novel by young generation as well as anyone who wants to be a humanitarian person. Through characters he chose, Sempiga powerfully and passionately shows that African countries should strive to end rampant wars and conflicts that have orphaned so many people and have led to poverty. This novel is simply a tender love story not just of one's parents but of one's country and continent."

-Sengabira Charmant,
visiting lecturer at Hankyong National University and Chairman of Rwandan Community in South Korea.


An excellent piece. It is a very creative way of expressing and interrogating one's deeper yearnings in a multi-faceted existential context: socio-economic, religious, family, culture, gender and political domains. Above all, the writing is a ray of hope in the midst of hopelessness!

-Daniel Mwamba Mutale, SJ


A very good piece of work!
The story reminds us of true stories from our past!

-Mr. Fabien Habimana,
Ministry of Education, Kigali-Rwanda
PhD Student at Beijing University of Chemical Technology
Beijing China

# Contents

To my late Father and Mother
– Christophe Hakizimana and Dative Nyirandegeya
– and to my siblings
– Jean Christophe Kanyarwanda, Olive
Nyirahakizimana and Oliviette Narame

I am grateful to many people whose support and encouragement allowed me to write this book. I am indebted to my late father Christophe Hakizimana who always believed in me and encouraged me to write books and to my late mother Dative Nyirandegeya who taught me to love and care for human beings. A very big thank you goes to my siblings – Jean Christophe Kanyarwanda, Olive Nyirahakizimana and Oliviette Narame– who have always been there for me and encouraged me when I was writing the book. Their life has been a great inspiration to me. *Un grand merci* to my wife Nadine Uwamahoro who was patient and supportive from the day she learnt about this project. I thank Jesuits who taught me, supported me and provided space as I began writing this book in 2012 when I was lecturing at Arrupe College in Zimbabwe. In a special way I thank Prof. Lawrence Daka, Prof. Simon Makuru and Prof. John Stacer who were my mentors and inspiration since I was a student at the same college. I am indebted to Prof. Anthony Chennells who guided me through my first steps of African and World Literature. I thank my students at Arrupe College who took the course on African Literature in French. It is indeed during this course that the idea to write this book came to my mind. I am grateful to Fathers Augustin Karekezi, Michel S. Kamanzi, Hugh Duffy and Mike Lewis of the Society of Jesus whose support to me and my siblings remains engraved in my heart. I will never forget the encouragement of Annonciata Nyiragwiza, Anne Marie Mukankuranga and Marie Mukabayiro, the three women who always treat me as their son. It will be a sign of ingratitude if I do not mention the unwavering support of aunt Donatille Mukarugwiza who took care of my siblings for a decade. My heart beats with gratitude to all those who have supported me financially for this book to be published. I am especially grateful to the Korean Government that offered me a scholarship to Dongguk University and to Ly Sophy. Dongguk University has become an academic home to me due to the support I always receive from Dr. Jong Guk Lee, Minsu Jang, Adriana Gabriela Quintero Romero, Prince-Arnaud Adiko and Tang Weinan. I appreciate the assistance of Dr Keith Essenther, Charmant N. Sengabira, Krista Nido, Patricia Kisaale, Lefani F. Mwanza, Ange Patrick D. and Daniel Mutale who read and commented on an early version of the book. While I acknowledge their immeasurable support, I take full responsibility for any shortcomings in the book.

# A life changing dream

It is 6 o'clock in the morning; sun rays are passing through Nadina's window in a beautiful fashion. Birds are slowly ceasing their beautiful songs that she has been enjoying for 30 minutes after waking up. The neighbourhood is still quiet; it is a perfect time for her to thank God for having protected her from wherever she was while asleep and to commend today's activities into his hands. She is well aware that many are those who sleep to never come back to life and disappear forever into the unknown world. Many are those in our insecure world who go to their daily routines never to return back home because of terrorism in trains, markets, airports, skyscrapers; almost in all corners of the world. Many are those who die of natural calamities like earthquakes and tornadoes while they had bright futures ahead of them and dreamt of becoming important people in the years to come.

Nadina is well familiar with all these natural calamities and man-made evil because as a journalist she reports on them on a regular basis. Sometimes she has to wake up in the middle of the night to go to the scenes. At times she does not even sleep at night when there is urgent news to prepare and report. Journalism is a job that she enjoys a lot because being a journalist was a dream come true. As a young girl,

Nadina had so many dreams. One of them is about fighting poverty and that is exactly why every morning she wakes up early and energetic hoping to realise her dreams one day. A person without a dream in his life does not need to wake up for he has no objective. Nadina having been born not just in a poor family but a poor country, wondered whether every humankind is poor but she was convinced it was a situation that could easily be overcome. After travelling to various places, she realised that there are people in the world who have beaten the trap of poverty. Her dream of fighting poverty even became bigger for she learnt some ways that could help in alleviating poverty. Even when she gets time to sleep sometimes she finds herself dreaming about having participated in activities aimed at reducing poverty. Every morning, before she gets out of bed she lies on the wall and jots down her dreams without stopping until she finishes. Afterwards, she closes her eyes to pray.

Unlike the usual, today, while she is trying to concentrate in prayer, a dream clearly stands out from the rest and keeps coming to her mind. It is a wonderful dream; the best dream in a long time. In the dream, the whole family, including her late mother and father, had gathered for the routine annual family feast. Everyone was happy to be there and to celebrate with others. Nadina was saddened to wake up and simply realise that it was just a dream. Strangely, due to this dream, she finds it hard to concentrate in her morning meditation. She can only pay attention to the ideas that run in her mind.

Although the dream is interfering with her prayers, she feels that the dream is becoming a source of happiness. This feeling of happiness coupled with sadness is a feeling that has never happened to her to such a degree. The dream is revealing to be a life-changing moment in her life. With this dream, she feels even closer to her late parents. For many years, she has been wondering how she could communicate with her father and mother who are on the other side of the river but when she thinks she has done it, she wakes up and she is always saddened to realise that she was dreaming. In a tone of disappointment she murmurs:

-   "Thanks to technology and science that have their main origin in the Enlightenment age, we now have boats, planes, vehicles, rockets, etc. that could help us reach almost anywhere within a short time. And now we have Internet whereby in a second, one click puts one into contact with a friend in hundred thousands of miles further."

She has been wondering whether science and technology are able to put us into contact with those on the other side of the river, those who have gone before us but science and technology are still disappointing in that regard. Even when they do put us in contact with the departed ones, it means something has gone wrong and for example an accident has taken place and hence one cannot come back once one crosses the river and enters into communion with those on the other side. The fact that one has to die for them to enter into communication with their ancestors discourages humankind very much and keeps them in despair, isolation and distant from the land of the living dead. Nadina hopes scientists will in the future discover easy and safe ways to communicate with our loved ones who went before us. Just like other journalists, Nadina has reported on people who claim to have died and come back to life and have told all sorts of stories on what goes on there in the other side of this life of ours. But she has always found the stories of these people hard to believe. Although she cannot believe these people she seems convinced that death is not the end of the journey. It is at the same time a continuation of the journey on earth but a beginning of another special journey to a different kind of life that we fail to grasp and describe. No wonder in her society people describe dying as passing on to the other side of the river or crossing the river.

Since she cannot concentrate in her meditation and only keeps thinking about how to communicate with her ancestors, she decides to get out of bed and get ready for work. She hopes today will turn out to be one of the best days having been indirectly entertained by her parents and rekindled the joy of being among them. Of her mother, she still has memories of how she used to take them to Church on Sundays after having dressed them in a smart way. After Church she could cook delicious fish. The fish was so delicious that even other kids from the neighbourhood would queue to be served. Nadina and her siblings would fight for the head of the fish for they had heard a myth that if one eats the head of a fish one is most likely to become intelligent. Some siblings still tease her that she has become intelligent because she has eaten many of those heads. After a nice meal they would go to play with other kids from their schools or the neighbourhood. As for her father, he was a hardworking man. Unfortunately working hard does not always make one rich. Despite not being very rich, Nadina remembers very well that their father loved them so much. She remembers that every Friday, her father would bring bread with him on his bicycle so that they could eat it over the weekend and by so doing have a little taste of how kids from rich families in their neighbourhood were living every day. Nadina misses her parents so much and would give everything she has to meet them once again. Their love and support were the best thing she ever had and are what she misses the most. But she cannot afford to be entangled with the sadness and emptiness created by her parents' departure. She has a mountainous task of taking care of her siblings.

Nadina has 4 siblings. Every day before taking shower, she promised them a phone call to check on them. It is the only way to show them that though far away physically her mind and heart are always with them. She hopes they also have dreams that wake them up each morning and that they long to fulfil those dreams one day. After the phone call to her siblings, she takes a shower and prepares her son to go to kindergarten and prepares breakfast for her husband. After sharing breakfast her husband drives her to work. On Saturdays and Sundays, her husband has begged her to rest and has volunteered to prepare breakfast! But actually she knows no weekend for most of the times there is work to do on weekends. There is a lot of news to report on. She believes that if one wants to stop poverty, injustice and inequality one ought not to rest.

# Communication with the other world

～•～

The dream scenario seems to have played the role of preparing an even more important discovery. Recently, Nadina discovered that for her to be able to share her stories with beings who are on the other side, she does not have to die. Neither does she have to hear from them through dreams for her to be in communion with them. The dream old-fashioned way of communication with the living dead is unfair for it is a one-way process. It saddens her to always remember that in spite of getting advises from, say, her father she is unable to respond to his generosity and love in tangible ways.

As if electronic engineers had been listening to her complaints a scientific breakthrough has been achieved. She is happy to read in the news that "from now onwards emails can be sent to the other side of the river where all those loved ones, enemies, good leaders and great dictators alike live; emails will also be received; all this in a matter of seconds". This means that her communication with her parents is going to be revived. She puts her thumbs up to the person who made this communication possible. Nadina is sure that the person who made this paradigm shift in technology had such a dream and could not rest until he had discovered a special way of communicating with his loved ones who are in another world. Although he may have stood on the shoulders of those who tried before him in vain and who had the same dream, destiny has made it that it is him who finally discovers the way we can communicate with those who are no more in our world but live on in the other. Now we can benefit from the fruits of his labour. All secrets and questions we have been keeping will be decoded. Nadina hopes in the near future people from the other side will also start using more sophisticated technology so that she could see her father's and mother's new faces and they could see how she has turned into a mother and has been blessed with a son. She is convinced that her parents will be more than happy to see and talk to their grand-child.

It is on the 16$^{th}$ 16 16. Numerologists tells us that this is a special day, a once in a lifetime day. As usual, she wakes up early in the morning, but instead of meditation, she decides to write her first ever email to her father. She stretches out her hand to reach out to her laptop. It was a newly acquired Samsung laptop that her husband had bought when he attended a seminar on Saemaul Undong in Seoul, South Korea. She holds the white machine in her soft hands.

She mumbles,

- I hope my stories will please and console my father even if, I suppose, it cannot add anything to the ultimate happiness that he has already appropriated. For all these years, I missed my father I have been wondering how I could tangibly get in touch with him just the same way I used to write to my boyfriend and now husband when he was studying in Europe. I was always frustrated that I was unable to talk to my dad and tell him once more how I miss him and how much I love him.

She starts touching laptop key board as fast as possible, writing whatever news comes to her mind hoping to edit her stories before clicking the send button.

*Dear Father Hachris,*

*What an historic day, what a joy to wake up one day and discover that it is possible to communicate directly to you despite the fact that I am unable to see you face to face and that you are no longer among the living of this world. I do not know where to begin my story from. I am at loss to explain to you how much we have been missing you. Truly no one ever can fill the gap you have created in our family. No one can heal the scars caused by your untimely departure. But we have tried to stay strong in the hope that we shall meet you once again. All your four children plus myself have grown very well, both in wisdom and physical appearance. I am no longer a teenager like the time when you left me; I no longer think like a child, I do not act like children anymore. I am no longer a child among my siblings. I have grown to become not only their mother but also and mainly their father, and I am proud of what I have accomplished. I do not pretend to have taken and accomplished your role and responsibility for no one can do. You are such a unique dad, you had a wonderful and big heart that no one else has in this world. The other world where you live has gained such an important personality but at the same time it was such a huge loss to our world. Thank you for giving me inspiration. Thank you for trusting me, thank you for encouraging me even when you are on the other side. Thank you for having given birth to me and siblings to take care of. It was never going to be an easy journey without you, but we are half way from where you left us. Your generosity and love have carried us through, your wisdom has lightened our darkness, your intelligence has opened our horizons, your heart has inspired our steps. Your absence has created a drive in our hearts to move on* and has doubled our efforts to compete in this world, a Darwinian jungle where we would surely die off if we remained weak and allowed the strong to feed on us. We refused to allow the strong to engulf us. The road was slippery but we managed to make strides, it was full of bumps and turns; full of hills and thorny grasses but we courageously moved on. At times we did not see ahead of us but we moved in trust and hope that we would not hit a dead end. Remembering how you always woke up early in the morning going off to work and you would always come back tired for our sake allowed us to soldier on. Resilience became of guide and support. Courage became the word that our lips uttered every morning. Perseverance became our morning prayer. Unity among ourselves remained a pillar. We allowed virtue to triumph on vice for the battle was difficult. There was surely no room for error and no time for mistake. The world we were fighting was stronger than us but we were wiser than it and we are on our way to victory even though the journey is still long.

Mbanda, your namesake, recently graduated from the National University and is proud to be part of the family. It has been a long and challenging journey for him but he is happy to have completed it. He has now come to understand what, in your wisdom, you used to tell him that life is not a straight line but rather a line with many curves, a journey with twists and turns in which one has to remain strong, patient, courageous and resilient in order not to fall down or drown in the mud and get stuck. Life is full of traps and one has to be clever to remove them. One should never give up. One should never back down because of challenges. Mbanda never imagined that he would attend a university in life if it were not for the generosity of the government and its donors who have been supporting students from humble backgrounds to get a decent education. Unfortunately, conditions through which Mbanda did his high school studies were not really favourable for him to get a scholarship from the government. One needed to get *good grades to obtain the government scholarship. Each morning before going to school Mbanda would first go to fetch water from a hill situated miles from home. After that he would work on the farm for one hour before heading to school. He always looked tired. These activities carried out before school definitely affected his academic performance. Every evening I tried to explain some course materials to him but he always felt sleepy. I do not think it was because Mbanda was lazy and did not love school but he worked so hard on the field so that we could have food to eat. Not just to our surprise but to that of Mbanda –Mbanda joined the rank of university degree holders despite coming from a poor background and working in harsh conditions.*

*As you remember, from the very beginning, generally children of the rich people go to good schools and children of the poor go to poor schools and that also may affect children the whole of their lives. Poor people study in very poor conditions with no (good) books, no (good) teachers etc. It is like the gospel being fulfilled that the poor will always be with us and those who have will be given more but those who have little even the little they have will be taken away from them. As you know in your time, many were those poor people who went to school where there was no school but just a tree to hide one's face from the sunshine. Of course there are poor people who go through difficult times and grow up to become powerful individuals but those are only few, an exception to the rule. Just like some kids from rich families throw away the opportunity of studying in good schools and become lazy and end up living a miserable life to an extent that some even commit suicide. But these are also exceptions. The world seems to be divided into the strong and the weak, the rich and the poor, us and them, them and us.*

*In her wisdom, and not desperation, my only grandmother tells me that as time passes, the world keeps becoming like a Darwinian Jungle where the rich and the powerful seem to flourish and most of the times exploit the weak and the poor who continue languishing in abject poverty. Each time we wake up to a world of selfish and power-hungry human beings, a world of inequality. She keeps reminding me of how she owned a big chunk of land in our city and how she is now languishing in poor conditions. She tells me that when people migrated to the city she gave them a big part of her land, and sold another part to others cheaply but all these people have turned a blind eye to her woes. To make matters worse, the government has taken the other part with very little compensation for unlike before the land belongs to the state. This land acquired by the government is situated in a strategic place and thus the government will make more money once the investors it wooed come and buy the land. My grandmother now struggles to get her traditional cigar while those she enriched regularly pass her every morning and evening in flashy vehicles without greeting her.*

*Yesterday, when my grandmother came to visit my siblings she was happy to find me at our ancestral house. As usual, she was carrying her walking stick. Her white hair always combed in a so nice and special way that we always like touching and looking at it when she comes home. She looked gorgeous even though the weight of age could be seen on her beautiful face. Her mind is still sharp and she suddenly recognized me. We chatted for a long time. I am always happy to learn from her wisdom. She has always been one of my role models.*

Nadina and her grandmother had a nice conversation which she remembers very well:

- My daughter you have become so beautiful just like your mum. Where do you live now?, Nadina's grandmother asked.
- Thank you grandma. I really miss my beautiful mother. And I am sure you miss her too. Last week it was mother's day. While my friends celebrate and give flowers to their

mother, I miss my mother even more. I cry and ask the world why it has taken her so early and why it has chosen her, Nadina replied fighting back her tears.

- I miss my daughter so much. As you know she was the only daughter I had. She was a woman of virtues and she respected our culture and elderly people. She was too good to live long on this earth. She assisted so many people while she was still alive. But I was surprised that all these people became strangers to your family once she died. No one even dared to help you. People no longer assist each other like when I was young; they seem only preoccupied by their self-interest. They keep becoming selfish, and I wonder what it will be like by the time you reach my age; my grandmother told me yesterday.

- Things change grandma. They can definitely not remain the way they were in your youth. Of course there is change for the better and change for the worse. It is sad that some people change for the worse and become corrupt and selfish instead of striving to leave the world better than they left it. It is a pity that selfishness keeps growing in our global village. What do you expect if what they care about is only themselves? Nadina retorted.

- Oh my granddaughter, you have really become wise. I love watching you and listening to what you tell people on Television. I am really proud of you. It is a sign that you care a lot about the progress of this nation and its people. You desire a world in which people help each other –a just, equal and peaceful world. I wish you to become someone more important than you are so that you will be able to bring about this kind of world you wish people to live in. She added.

As Nadina is about to type another word on the message to send to her father, her little boy starts crying. The boy is only 1 year and 2 months. When he is not hungry he is always quiet, he likes people and never fears them like some other babies. Each time he cries, Nadina knows the boy most likely wants to be breastfed unless her body temperature indicates that he is not feeling well or that he wants his clothes changed in case he has urinated in them. After realising that he wants to be breastfed, Nadina breastfeeds him for a couple of minutes. The little boy becomes quiet and then after some minutes of playing with his mum falls asleep. Nadina takes her laptop once more. She realises that her son interfered with the speed at which ideas were flowing. She has even forgotten what she was talking about in her last line before he interrupted her. She scrolls up to remind herself. Ideas come again. Even if the email is so long, she has no intention to stop yet. She hopes that his father and all those on the other side have enough time in their hands and that they are not like us who at times wished we had a day of more than 30 hours.

*Dear father, initially I used to believe that without a scholarship award no one in our family would have gone to school but I will explain to you how I was mistaken when I tell you the miraculous education of my sisters. Before I do that let me tell you how Mbanda surprised himself and ourselves. In his first attempt in the A level national exam, Mbanda passed but having obtained 4.4 grades out of 10 he failed to secure the government scholarship because only someone who got at least 4.8 in their group was supposed to win the scholarship award. He believed that if one has to live a decent life in this country and in our global world, one will have to be at least a university graduate, nothing less. He therefore decided to sit the national exam for the second time without necessarily going back to school. The National*

Examination Council would keep him grades of courses which he passed well in the first attempt and will add them to the courses he would attempt for the second time.

There were two options for people like Mbanda; to go back to school or to be private candidates who are not attached to any school but directly to the National Examination Council. Mbanda chose the latter for he did not have school fees for an entire school year. The little money we had was used to pay for his sisters as I will tell you later. Many people wondered whether he would pass the exams and get a scholarship he failed to get while in school where he had teachers teaching and guiding him, with a library at school no matter how poor it was and enough time to revise.

To register to the National Examination Council, one has to pay a certain amount of money; as you know there is no free lunch in this world. Unfortunately, Mbanda did not have US$ 50 required for one to register as a private candidate in the National Examination Council and hence be allowed to write the exam. He did not know what to do to obtain the money. All those he asked for a loan told him that they had some problems at home and therefore were not in position to assist him. Maybe my grandmother was right yesterday that people no longer assist one another. Maybe people have problems of their own. Mbanda thought he would have to wait for the following year. But that was if National Examination Council would still keep the private candidates programme running since many departments in this country keep changing depending on which ministers are appointed. Knowing that passing the exams and getting a scholarship is a once in a life time chance and that he was not getting younger, on the last day of registration, my other brother –Mzee – got an idea, only God knows from where, and advised Mbanda to get the money from a neighbour with whom Mzee had spoken on the phone. Mzee had promised to pay back the neighbour with a certain interest when *he comes back from abroad where he was studying. Mbanda did get the money and was quick to inform Mzee that he registered and at the same time thank him so much for assisting him.*

*In the meantime, Mbanda got a job of cooking at a restaurant in a city where I was studying. This job was so demanding that he hardly found time to revise let alone to rest. He would spend the whole day and part of the night cooking or serving customers. While other workers would be resting, he would be revising. He slept for three hours a day from the time he got the job to the time he sat for his exams. He looked exhausted and I always wondered whether he would get enough strength to write his exam and pass well above the required note for obtaining a government scholarship.*

*When exam time was around the corner, Mbanda requested to go on leave from his employer so that he could sit for the national exams that he virtually was never prepared for.*

- *Could you please give me two weeks' leave so that I can prepare for my national exams and write them? He told his employer.*
- *Exams? Which exams young man? Since when did you become a student? The employer told him angrily.*
- *I am a private candidate at the National Examination Council. I am supposed to write exams this time around so that I can obtain a government's scholarship! Mbanda said.*
- *Poor kids make me laugh! You have two choices young man. You either go to write your exam and you get no salary for this month or you stay here and work! This is a private company; all that interests us is money! Do you hear me? The employer retorted.*
- *Yes sir! I have to write the exam. This exam is my future. I would rather quit so that in the future I can get a better job. Mbanda told the boss.*

- *Ok. I will not give you two weeks, you only have one week to write exams. You may now get out of my office. Remember that you will not get your salary for this month if you miss that week.*

*Mbanda never told the employer that he was a student for had he told him, he would not have been employed in the first place. As a matter of fact, Mbanda was advised not to tell his employer that he was a private candidate for if he did he was not going to obtain the very job just like it happened to some people who applied for the job in the past. People who worked with that employer knew how tough and arrogant he was and advised Mbanda to just wait for the time for exams and request for permission.*

*Since he desperately needed the job he decided to combine it with being a student. Having realised that he had little time to revise, Mbanda's confidence and hope that he would get more marks than the ones he got in his first attempt and thereby obtain a scholarship started to fade. He actually feared he would get lower marks. If banking marks through National Examination Council was not an option, he would have even thought he would fail. Hoping against odds, he just decided to do his best even if his best this time around may be worse than his best in the first attempt.*

*Even if confidence and hope had started to fade, courage has always been Mbanda's faithful companion and pillar. Courage accompanied him when it was time for exams. When he finished his exams he called me. Like many students do he insisted the exam was tough. Lacking confidence and hope, he thought there was no way he was going to pass. But his heart was divided. When he thought of the courage with which he embraced this task all along, from preparation to writing the exam, part of his heart would have a glimpse on victory. I asked him to wait patiently for the publication of the results. In the meantime, he could concentrate on his mini-job even though he unjustly lost a well-deserved monthly salary. Ironically, that month his picture hang everywhere as the employer of the month. There is no doubt that the salary was released only to end up in the pockets of the boss. Mbanda's salary is definitely less than a tenth of the manager's salary but the latter cannot let the opportunity of getting what belongs to my brother slip away. One wonders till when those who have power will stop abusing it and abandon exploiting powerless poor. The powerful, the mighty may be always considered right but mighty may be madness at times if it is abused and used to exploit the weak and needy. Power normally is given us to assist those who do not have it and not the other way round but few are those who comprehend its purpose and use it wisely and to the benefit of those it is meant to benefit. Our teachers always insisted that power should be used to bring about the good of the community and should never be abused. Mbanda decided not to complain about his salary to higher authority because he knows that the authorities will always take the side of his boss even if the latter is at fault. He just enjoyed the honor of being employee of the month although in the first place he does not work hard to get prizes or any award of the sort.*

*Three months later results were released by National Examination Council. Unlike during our time today it is possible to check results on the Internet but since there is no internet connection in the village where my brother lives he has to go to district office to check results on the notice board. I thought this could turn out to be one of the most important days for Mbanda and so decided to accompany him to check the results. Many white papers hanged on the board and a few on the walls since they could not fit on the notice boards available. Many students turned up for the occasion. While some were smiling for having succeeded others were crying because they had failed. Mbanda was shivering and one could see on his face that he was afraid that the worse may be coming. We stared at the wall where the white papers hanged. To my surprise, I realised that he had obtained the same grade, 4.4 like in the first attempt. I pointed at his name and grade and he looked at them and he made a sigh of relief having recalled tough times that he experienced in the run up to the second attempt. We had a nice conversation of which I kept a record.*

- *Thank God I did not get lower marks but my hope of going to the university is most likely shuttered. Probably it is not meant for me! I feel guilty that I wasted Mzee's money. I lost my salary in vain. He immediately said to me.*

*Wiping a tear on my cheek, I struggled to speak as I embraced him and congratulated him. But congratulating him for what? I asked myself. Maybe I congratulated him for not having failed; for having obtained that mark in harsh conditions with no teacher to guide him, no library to do research, no time to revise.*

- *Dear brother, I know how hard you worked trying to accomplish your job and revise for the exam. I cannot but congratulate you for your efforts and courage in difficult moments. I know that if you had had enough time to revise and study you would have had higher grade than that. It is unfortunate that you combined revision and the job. Maybe this is a sign that you shouldn't have continued to work after you registered in National Examination Council! I added in a sympathising voice but not convinced with my last sentence.*
- *So what would I have done? He replied, sounding agitated. That means I was supposed to go back to school.*
- *Probably you could have considered going back to school to have enough time and resources to prepare for the exams. I retorted.*
- *But where would I have gotten school fees? Sister, you are not being fair. You remember that I struggled to even get*

*the 50 dollars to register in the National Examination Council; you remember how I struggled to pay for my school fees when at school. They always sent me back home to get the remaining fees and I would spend weeks at home waiting for fees I do not know from where. Remember: both Mzee and you did all you could to make me study while no one among you was working. I did not want to trouble anyone anymore. In fact, there is no evidence that had I gone to school I would have had more marks than now. Dear sister, I know you are a student at the university with so much to attend to, with little pocket money even for your needs and therefore it would have been too much for you to pay for my school fees. I knew I would need little money to buy myself new clothes, to get bus fare and to attend to other needs. To achieve this I needed to work fulltime. Maybe I should not have gone to work in the restaurant where I had no time to revise and no time to sleep. But where could I have worked since that was the only place available at that moment? I was even very lucky to get employed there.*

- *You are absolutely right brother, hiding my embarrassment at how he knows the reality we live in, I added; it is not easy to get a job in this country especially when you are a high school graduate. Time is coming fast when even people with university education will struggle to find jobs. The government never publishes the rate of those who are unemployed for fear that people would react angrily at the statistics. But in any case, people are already aware that the number of unemployed is very high and it is more than urgent to reduce this number.*

*Our conversation reminded me of tough times Mbanda went through when he did high school. He always had to work during holidays. High school students had two to three weeks of holiday for the first and second terms and a two month-holiday for the long break. When kids for the elite were resting and enjoying their holidays, Mbanda was busy inquiring where there is work. He was a minor but always carried out work of adults. Usually, he would work in construction sites as a helper to those who built schools or other buildings. He would mix cement, fetch water and carry bricks for them. He would also dig trenches where the construction was going to take place. That would require many calories and yet he would not have eaten very well. He was always a loser but he had to get a part of school fees for the following term to which Mzee and I would add the rest. Holidays were his Calvary for he would go back to school having lost much weight. While fellow students were unhappy to return to school for there were no eggs and meat for example he would be graduated to two meals a day and did not have to labour like he did during holidays.*

*After confirming the results together, we concluded that Mbanda was never going to the university in the foreseeable future. There was no way he was going to quit the job so that he studies full-time. Not only was he sure that this third time he was going to pass but also he was helping Mzee and I to pay bills at home. However, as one African proverb goes,* God always watches over a poor man. *When scholarships were published, Mbanda decided to check how many of his former schoolmates obtained scholarships and to which schools they had been sent. As he was reading the newspaper in which scholarship fellows were published he read Mbanda John won the scholarship award for that year. He was happy to learn that there was someone who bears exactly the same names who had passed. But he realised that the same Mbanda sat the exam for similar subjects, was an independent candidate and had obtained 4.4 out of 10 just like he did. He started to hope that he may be the one but he had no confidence yet. His courage was called upon once more: the only proof would be to check registration number, he quickly thought. Mbanda realised that this person had the same registration number like him. As he was thinking who this might be he received a call from Mzee congratulating him on securing a scholarship. Mbanda began to believe that he may have made it this time around. He told me that he cried a lot and failed to talk to Mzee. He does not remember the last time he had such kind of emotions. He thought he was dreaming or watching a movie.*

*Mbanda could not believe that he was among those who got the government scholarship. He thought this was a mistake. He later revealed to me that he read the list in the newspaper four times and had to call someone to read for him to ensure he was not dreaming. Of course a sceptic will have laughed at his method of justification and seeking for evidence from others because one can think he is calling the other person to verify for one even in a dream. After having regained his senses, Mbanda later called abroad to thank Mzee that his dollars had done the trick. In fact, he got his scholarship to arguably the best university in the country, the National University. Even if the standards of education in our country have fallen below the expected standards the National University to which Mbanda was sent is still reputable despite the fact that most of its professors are accused of not conducting enough research. Mbanda could not hide the fact that this was the happiest moment of his life. He was now ready to go back to school this time around in a different capacity and hoping to get out and get a better job than cooking and serving people food. Mbanda's dream was to become a professor to bring light to the dark age that engulfs his people. He believes education is still needed in his country if the people are to develop and to build strong institutions. Today like in the past institutions are weak for they depend on strong men that rule the country. Some of these leaders are not educated. Mbanda's goal is education for everyone especially poor kids in the village who miss on the chance of attending school not because they are ignorant and stupid but because they have no schools in their village or their parents do not care much about education having themselves not gone to school.*

*Mbanda spent four years at the university. It was a difficult journey. The scholarship offered by the government covered tuition fees, living allowance which helped him to carry out various activities like printing his notes, eating, accommodation, transport etc. The scholarship is offered in such a way to be paid 65% once Mbanda gets employed. A serious inconvenience by most students is that living allowance was almost all the time delayed. Sometimes it would come after three months, if at all. That means he would have to be patient and to seriously prioritise. Sometimes, it was wise to eat only once a day to save some money for other needs like buying clothes. Although there is no money that is ever enough, Mbanda's scholarship allowance was too little to cover his basic needs. But it would be a sign of ingratitude to keep complaining about the fact that the money is too little. Kids who get scholarships forget that many are those who struggle for years to find scholarships in vain. Others forget that besides the monthly allowance, tuition fees are paid and this constitutes the big chunk of the scholarship and indeed the bigger part of the scholarship.*

*During the four years he spent at the University, I realised that he has grown and has come to be a responsible and wise man that I love so much, admire and from whom I have learnt a great deal of things. From the time I left home, Mbanda has been taking care of everything and looks after our siblings at home since I cannot be there all the time. He is hard working and loves others. That is why I called my first born Mbanda, junior and asked Mbanda, senior, to be his God father when my son was baptised.*

*In fact, Mzee recently told me in a Skype conversation.*

- *That boy, Mbanda, always amazes me. He works hard. If it were possible, I would have given him my title as a first born.*

- *Well, we made him something close to being the head of the family, I said. He has access to the family's little money in the bank and we can entrust him any activities that bring progress to the family and we would be sure that he would do it quickly as if he has more hours than the rest of us. He has been looking after his siblings very well. I am glad he has followed what I taught him and has done it very well. He has taken a huge burden off my shoulders since last year, after many years of struggle. He says what he does is following in my footstep and in recognition of the good that I have done to the entire family.*

- *Yes I know that some of the family properties are written in his name and I am contemplating asking him to take even those that are still in my name. Even if I cannot in practice make him the first born, I told him that he has to take that role of the first born since most of the times I would be absent. Since then he never ceases to impress me. (Honestly, no one would deserve this title of first born more than you Nadina it is only that we live in a patriarchal society and a girl seems to be ignored), Mzee said.*

- *He has really taken that role very well. Impressive. I added.*

*While at the university, Mbanda initiated the idea or rather the project that would help us survive the hardships of Kayiga capital city and to pay for school fees of one of our sisters. He asked that we buy a taxi motorbike. Mzee sent some money from Rome and I added the little I had and Mbanda bought the bike. Unfortunately, the very first week the motorbike went on the road, it was involved in an accident. Mzee received a call informing him of the accident while he was conversing with his girlfriend Janet who had visited him at the campus. Janet told me how Mbanda's face changed completely as a sign of despair when he heard the bad news. He could not talk for some minutes. He wondered how the family was really going to survive and whether university education was over for his sister. He wondered where Mzee and myself would get other moneys to buy a new motorbike for this was partly the money Mzee spared for three years from his little pocket money.*

*Thank goodness the accident was not serious. The motorbike was repaired and went on the road once again. With the motorbike, children's life at home was no longer the same. They managed to eat a little bit well, to pay electricity bills and to install water at home, and to clothe themselves decently, all because of the ingenious ideas of Mbanda after some years of doing Project Management at the University. We could even afford to give some money to Mbanda as pocket money to cover up the gap caused by the fact that money from the government scholarship always delayed to come if at all it came.*

Nadina looks at her watch and realises that she is already running late to work. She knows it would take longer to get to work than the usual 20 minutes since her husband left already. She takes the phone and excuses herself to the boss saying that she will be a bit late. Nadina knows that she got too much excited with this new technology of communicating with the living dead. But she also knows that communicating with her father is a worthwhile experience and it is an inspiration in her quest of bringing about a better, just and equal world as her father has always been a mentor in this regard. Nadina puts down the phone and decides to conclude her email on this historic day.

*Dear father, it is a great pleasure writing to you after so many years. It reminds me of the time that I was in high school when I would send you letters via the rector of our school. Sometimes the letter would reach you with some news out-dated but I knew you would still be happy that I had taken the initiative to write you. I feel like I should keep telling you more news but if I continue you would not receive this email. I will tell you more stories tomorrow. I have to go and shower and prepare for work. We love you.*

*Yours ever loving you,*
*Nadina a.k.a Fille.*

Nadina cannot believe that she has written all these things. This is the longest email she has ever written.

- Even my husband never received such an email when he was doing his masters abroad, she recalls.

Nadina's husband wonders whether his wife is working on a book for he left her home in the morning when she was still composing the email. Normally when he realises that she is busy he does not disturb her for he knows that she can always take a bus to work although this rarely happens.

Nadina clicks on the send button and the computer reads: "Message sent to Hachris". This action pleases her very much. She is full of joy as she takes a bus to work.

Although she is happy, the day has turned out to be one of the longest in her life because she cannot wait to read from her father. As she is about to return home in the evening she realises that today she did not work as well as she would have loved because her mind was focused on the reply from her dad. She kept checking the email in vain. Her boss must have realised that there was something different with her not to say something wrong with her. Everyone could tell that despite the overexcitement she had she did not look in her usual and natural mood. Thank God it is one of the few days she does not have to appear on TV otherwise viewers would detect her agitations. She is also lucky that today she worked in the office and did not have to run upside and down to report on news in different localities. Until noon there was no response from the other world. Nadina started doubting the newly discovered technology and whether it is really true that message can cross over to the other side. She wondered whether it was because the concept of time could be different from the other side of the world in comparison to the way we view time.

As usual, in the evening, her husband comes to pick her from work. Dressed in a nice black suit with lines, a white shirt, a red neck tie and putting on black shoes, he looks great. He is not only handsome but he is charming and has a big and generous heart. Many women envy Nadina and cannot stop telling her how lucky she is to have married such a loving man. These women are well aware that the value of marriage for many people has been lost. It has become rare to see happily married couples who complement each other. Nadina and her husband enter their white Benz and rush home to get a well-deserved rest after such a hectic day in the office.

- Sweetheart, I hope you had a wonderful day in the office, Nadina asks her husband.
- Yes I did. Today we had a surprise visit from country manager of our bank. I showed him around and explained various things to him. He was very much pleased and satisfied on how our branch is doing. He praised our customer care. He is well aware that most banks in the country and most other branches of our very own bank are still lagging behind and do not seem to care much about customer care, Nadina's husband replied.

- It is a pity that banks let people queue for hours and sometimes when their turn is up they do not get the fair treatment they are supposed to. Some of my friends have actually changed banks in the hope of getting better customer care. It is a good thing that banks have built more branches but it is surprising that this has not changed much in customer care. Probably, it is in our culture to work slowly and neglect the other and not care much about time. It is as if we have more time than other races on other continents. I remember you told me how much you are impressed by Koreans who always do things fast as if they had 12 hours rather than 24. No wonder they developed quickly. Probably, our leaders need to emphasize on the attitude and the culture if we are to develop quickly. There seems no time to waste.

- Yes you are absolutely right. Our leaders have a lot on their plate. They need also to build more and bigger roads.

- The traffic jam is becoming common nowadays and it annoys me every time I go back home. Not only are our roads too small but people do not seem to follow the rules of the road. They just drive anyhow, Nadina tells her husband.

- It looks like everyone owns a car these days. Our roads have become even smaller compared to 10 years ago. There is need to find a quick solution to this problem. If our public transport was good there would normally be no need of taking personal vehicles. The environment would benefit from that as well. I wonder whether we will ever use the underground part of our land travelling to various destinations like developed countries have done, the husband replies.

- If they have managed it we can also manage it if we work hard. But we need radical change in almost all domains. We need good and visionary leaders to take us through that process.

Finally, they reach home and Nadina rushes to her laptop to check her emails. She was like a teenage girl who is in love and is longing to receive a message from her lover. Luckily she had to explain the whole saga to her husband so that he does not suspect that she is in love with someone else. It is becoming common for partners to suspect one another since nowadays many couples have sadly become unfaithful towards each other.

After opening her emails she shouts. Her father had just replied her email. She cannot believe her eyes. She is not sure whether to doubt. It may just be a figment of her mind. This reminds her of what the teacher told them in high school that what if the whole of our life was just a dream. It is like someone who is reading an interesting novel only to realise that he has been dreaming and not reading anything at all. But Nadina does not want to yield to this temptation. Meanwhile Nadina's husband has gone to the room to see how their boy is doing. He caresses him and plays with him. The boy has really missed him and is full of smiles. He usually enjoys playing with his dad. When Nadina's husband hears his wife shout, he comes running to see what had happened. Nadina has tears of joy and finds it hard to explain. He is surprised to see her in that over joyous mood. It is only a couple of minutes after they separated. She can only point to her laptop in disbelief. The boy is excited to see his mother but he is completely at loss. He ignores what is going on. Nadina asks her husband to sit down so that they can read together the email that has just come from the living dead.

# A breath-taking response

Nadina will never forget her father's charming response to her email! Indeed, although a quiet man, whenever he spoke people would always find wisdom at work in him. They always came to him to speak of their burdens and he was always there to listen and counsel. Nadina has taken on this role and it fits well with her job of journalists. But not only does she not have time for that but she has not acquired enough wisdom yet and the calmness that characterised her father.

*Dear Nadina, thank you very much for your wonderful email. What a tremendous joy it was to hear from you again. When our Leader on this other side of the river realised that there was no way people from your side could respond to communication you received from us through dreams and other methods, He decided to adopt your own simple way of communication and allowed one genius man on your side to discover how communication from your world to ours is possible using the existing technology on your side. I am sure you would wonder why it took many centuries for humankind to establish such a relationship. I guess you also have an answer for the question for it is simply because the world develops in a certain direction and at a certain pace and it took human beings so long to achieve the level of technology that it takes for you to enter into contact with us. It would be stupid to ask why humans in the age of Plato could not make planes or why people in the time of Shakespeare did not ride in tubes as we know them today in London Underground. There is no doubt that with time and success of this new method, other methods will be developed. What a breakthrough this is for you people.*

*I am more than pleased to read your email and to get the news of some of my children. Allow me to tell you that when I read that Mbanda managed to go the university and you are married with one son I was very excited. I laughed to the extent that many beings here came to see me for they wondered what had happened to me. I was one of the first beings here to receive an email from the other side and so they thought that was the reason. However, it is because of the good news of Mbanda and you. Congratulations! I cannot but be proud of you. Well done kids! I always had a feeling you were going to make it no matter how tough it would be. The first day I arrived here I went straight to our Leader to meet him and express my concern.*

- Look! You called me too early in my fifties. I had 5 children to take care of. I had lots of ambitions to fulfil. I had lots projects to make the world a better place. By the way why did you take my wife long time ago and left me alone? Don't you have feelings? Don't you realise that it is hard in our poor country to raise kids alone especially as a man? Now you have allowed them to remain on their own. At Church, they always told us that you are omnipotent, that you know everything and that you are ever good and loving. But the wars and conflicts that have torn our country since I was a kid have made me to doubt these qualities and qualifications attributed to you. If you are omnipotent why did you allow the war to take place? Why do you allow people to be so selfish and fight each other? Why do you allow my wife to die so young? Why do you allow my children to struggle? If you are omniscient why did you create our country different from our neighbouring countries and you gave us no natural resources, no fertile lands to work on? Why did you allow our race to appear inferior everywhere it goes? Are you really good and loving? I will not ask you anymore question for these are more than enough. If you are really all those things, take care of my children. Give peace to my country. Stop corruption and endless poverty and conflicts.

-    ….

*I did not get any response. My Leader just smiled and patted my shoulders. After that gesture, he hugged me as if to welcome me and console me. I knew he was very sympathising to my situation. But I still wonder whether he has all those qualities we attribute to him. May be he has those qualities and the problem is us who fail to grasp it.*

-    Welcome to this world of bliss. With time you will understand how loving I have always been but how much this love I have for you has limited my omnipotence and restricts my omniscience.

*I have no idea if telling you the first encounter with my leader helps you but it helped me pour out my anger on him. I have come to understand many things since then and with time I will find simple ways to explain some of the realities with you although I am aware that you cannot grasp everything despite the fact that I know that you are a very intelligent lad. In any case, I am glad that you guys have grown and are happy. By now, due to difficult experience that you underwent, you have learnt that having and being are definitely different things. Having or possessing things is good but does not necessarily have anything to do with being free, being happy, being reasonable, being a truly human being who thinks of and cares about his fellow human beings. What matters is not how much money you possess but how kind you are as a person and how you use your possession to assist others. I actually understood it more as I crossed the river and reached the other side of your world. You remember I left without almost anything apart from my clothes and the two gifts Mzee gave me (thank him on my behalf by the way). Many are those who tore to accumulate assets thinking they will bring them happiness but few are those who are truly happy despite possessing the whole world. Some people seem to think that they will cross the river with their belongings and properties. Others do not believe that there is life beyond there and so amass riches by hook and crook as they want to enjoy to the fullest. But unfortunately, they cannot fill the void in their hearts. The more they get the more they want. The more they want the more they get blind and start to get corrupt and so exploit the fellow human beings. Some even kill to possess the belongings of others. Riches never seem to be enough.*

*I am glad that you guys have focused more on being rather than having. Even though having is an important aspect of your lives, you should not let it take over from who you are. You could have had more things than you have but that would not necessarily have taught you how to treat your siblings better. Neither will it necessarily make you relate to fellow humans better. You know people –including members of our family – who have a lot and once their brothers and sisters die they torment their children that they want what belonged to their relatives as if what they have is not enough for their well-being. Those are never happy for they confuse being with having. They confirm that human beings never get satisfied. Each person no matter how much they possess want to possess even more. But truly happy are they who are satisfied with what they have and possess and happy with who they are. This does not mean that they cannot and should not work hard to have more or become better but they do this believing that this is* an excess. They would still be happy with what they have. They learn that the world does not revolve around them alone. Therefore, they do not benefit alone they allow others to benefit as well. I am glad that you have managed very well with the little you have simply because it conglomerates with the good character that has developed in you. Not having anything is like a curse also. You need to have the minimum required for you to be who you are also. Therefore, we should not forget the minimum relationship between the two. If Mbanda did not have the 50 dollars he received from Mzee he would not be where he is today. If you guys did not work hard to possess what you have you would have lived a miserable life. That is why I always encouraged you in your dream of eradicating poverty, a dream that you had since you were a little kid. I hope you still nourish and cherish that dream and have started turning it into reality.

It is consoling indeed to hear that Mbanda has grown into a pleasing and responsible young man. Tell him that I am still proud of him and congratulate him on his university achievements. Tell him to be happy of those achievements. Despite all he has achieved, he needs to remain a humble and loving gentleman. He should not trample on his enemies simply because he has achieved what he always dreamt of. Even those who could not help him when they could; he should help them together with their children whenever they are in need. The difficult experience through which he lived should be a great teacher in his life who asks him to take care of all those people suffering in that country in one way or the other especially the orphans and poor of all kinds.

Dear Nadina, greet everyone on my behalf. Tell them that we (you mother and myself) miss you a lot. This message is just a foretaste of what is still to come. I will explain more things little by little. Peace and Love.

Your ever loving father,
Hachris.

# Unexpected Uniting Death

Nadina is very excited to receive a quick reply from her father on the other side. Definitely, the joy is not as if she is seeing him again but it is one of the greatest moments of her life. Every morning, after the routine phone call to her siblings, she sends her father a message. That means that she has to wake up earlier than she normally used to. She has now become a mediator between her siblings and their parents since they do not easily access the sophisticated technology. Not only do they neither have powerful phones nor laptops to access the Internet; but also they do not have money to be able to connect since Internet is still expensive in their country. In fact, it takes more money to reach those who are the other side of the river than it would take sending an email to someone from another continent. But the wonderful message she received from her father proves that it is worth paying for. She will get to know a number of things from her father and probably to unlock the secrets of death and suffering that human beings have to endure. She will use her skills of a journalist to disseminate this new knowledge and information in an effective and fast manner. She has now started asking herself a host of questions.

- I wonder what kind of computers they use on the other side of the world. Do they have bodies? Are they just spirits? Do they live together? What kind of transformation did they undergo? Is it everyone who dies who goes where they are or just a selected few? Is it everyone who is able to communicate with their loved ones? Will we recognize them when we get there and vice versa? What kind of place and environment do they live in? Is it another planet? I hope my dad will be able to answer the journalistic questions that always pop into my mind once I start interviewing people of all careers and backgrounds, she noted in her diary.

It is another day, the weather has suddenly changed. It has been raining the whole night. The breeze from the east is blowing; birds did not sing they seem to be hiding from the rain in their nests. It looks like it is going to rain again. Nadina takes her computer again. She is sure that as long as her husband is aware of what is going on she feels safe. But her husband does not seem as excited as she expected him to be for he suspects that hackers are fooling her around. He says that there is no way those from the other side could enter into communication with us. He adds that even dreams are not actually communication but what is in our subconscious. It is just our desires and imagination that we project. Nadina is convinced that it is difficult if not impossible to try to convince someone if they do not believe something. With time she will know whether her husband is right or not. She is not in any way discouraged by what her husband tells her about communication with her father. She starts writing again despite nurturing a little doubt.

*Dear father,*

*Thank you very much indeed for your amazing reply. After laying your corruptible body in the compound in Narame, where you were born, I believed that your soul remains incorruptible. I have no way of proving it. I just believe. And maybe I do not need any proof whatsoever, I am the proof itself. More so I was convinced that inspiration could be drawn from your immortal soul even after your body was laid to rest. I requested you and pleaded with you, insisting that I should never be led to shame by failing to raise my siblings. I knew that Mzee could not do it, having joined a religious congregation and having taken a vow of poverty, and so the burden and more so the responsibility was on my shoulders. I know many people were wondering what was going to happen to us. So was I —more than anyone. But as events turned out, they were wrong in their worries no matter how difficult the current struggle in life may be.*

*When the burial was over, I remained alone at your grave for some minutes. I knelt down, not just in tears but with confidence, praying and pleading with you. I remember having uttered and murmured, "Shame on you, father, if you ever let me down in this new and difficult responsibility you decided to give me prematurely. Shame on you if you ever let me down and forget to continue looking after your children. Look! I am still a student at the university; I have barely begun my first year. Soon I will get married and look after my husband and family and now you leave me like that! Why did you not wait for us all to get married and become independent? Why did you leave me with this insurmountable mountain? Why did you allow our friend death to take you so early before you accomplish your responsibilities? Did you give birth to me so that I suffer? You knew very well that our lovely mother was no more and you decided to go. Suddenly, and just like that. Your body was not listening but your soul, your spirit, your shadow was —I was convinced. You were not dead but had undergone a deep transformation and transfiguration through which we shall also pass come our time.*

*Some of our enemies touched each other and looked at me in mockery when I stayed at the grave in silence and disbelief. They wondered what I was doing there and concluded it was a pure sign of desperation and fetishism. They said that a girl isn't going to manage taking care of her siblings. I knew I would not count much on any other person since they also have their insurmountable problems and most of those who do not have these problems have become egoists. Indeed, as my grandmother has wisely put it people do not longer assist each other as they used to. I asked you for whatever it takes, as if you were the provider of things, as if, once dead and transformed, you had acquired super powers and more things than when alive, things that you would provide to me so that I could be able to take care of my siblings. I was convinced you would do something. I did not despair. In any case my dream of fighting poverty did not end with your death it only grew stronger. It had just begun. Indeed "what does not kill me makes me stronger". I always remember this line of Viktor Frankl in his Man's Search for Meaning, when I despair and search for meaning in difficult and hard times. I had to focus on the family problems first and foremost and I knew in your absence the ball was in my court and I had to play it and play it wisely. I was ready to win through countless challenges. You have always provided an inspiration and even if I despaired I also had the courage to follow in your footsteps knowing that you will never abandon me and that you would never leave with me a task impossible to accomplish.*

*I left the grave with a surprise of joy and with a feeling that you had listened to my plea and prayer. Even if you did not have the power to do anything much at least you would intercede for me from those you find on the other side. I was convinced that your example while on earth will be always a great teacher. From that* joy, I drew energy to soldier on and to comfort my siblings. I knew that my new and mountainous responsibility had started. From then onwards, I had to combine university studies, taking care of my siblings and marriage preparations. I was sure that whenever the goings get tough I would come to this grave to cry and to plead with you so that you would assist me. After everyone had gone back to their homes, I felt alone and on my own. I did not feel the presence of my siblings. You left a great void not just in our hearts but in our house. Things were never going to be the same without your quiet and charming presence. It is like the world crumbled on me. I had no energy, I could not feel my joints anymore, it is like I had ceased to exist. I was in this world without being there. I felt completely lost without your support and love. It was like the end of the world for me. All this feeling took place before I was told that very night that you said that you are happy to go to the land of the living now that Nadina has grown up and will undoubtedly take care of her siblings. I wonder where you got that confidence and insight knowing that I had no job and I was getting ready to take up new responsibility with my own family. I wonder why you would wish to leave me such a mountainous task, knowing the path our first born had chosen. Having joined religious life, Mzee, was in no way going to take on the role of taking care of us.

In any case, thank you for trusting me, thank you for believing in me, thank you for making me discover my talents, for allowing me to take initiatives. Indeed, thank you for allowing me to continue from where you stopped. Thank you for allowing me to be where you are not physically. Thank you for being such an inspiration. Thank you for teaching our society that a girl child can also perform well like her brother. Supported by the love I had learnt from you, the courage that I sucked from my mother's breast, the steadiness that I learnt since in my mother's womb and the generosity you and my mother taught me, the resilience from my school teachers and the trust from my husband-to-be, the *support and incomparable love of my siblings, the wisdom from my grandmother, the care from my mother-in-law to be, I embarked on the long journey of taking care of my siblings. I was aware that I was supposed to accomplish that task not just as the second born but from then onwards as the father and mother of my siblings.*

*Initially, I put on hold my marriage preparations and thought I should postpone marriage indefinitely. I knew that if I ever get a job, I would not be free to do what I want with my money especially helping my siblings because then the money will be for my new family. I talked it over with my fiancé but he suggested that postponing our marriage indefinitely would be suicidal.*

- *Your father is late and you have children to take care of but that should not be the reason why you should abandon all your life projects. He retorted.*

- *I am scared for the future of my siblings and I feel there is a lot to be done since all of them are still in school and will even have to go to the university. You know in our country with only a high school degree one may never get a job. Therefore, I need more years to take care of them before I can think about getting married. I still love you and will keep loving you even in the four years or so to come, and I hope and pray it remains the same with you. I said fighting back my tears.*

- *Ma chérie, he always called me, I do not think that this is the way to go. We need to keep thinking about marriage and prepare ourselves in consequence. Of course we will not wed this year as initially planned since we will be mourning your father but most probably next year. We have to say goodbye to being bachelors as soon as we can. The earlier we get married the better. Your family is my family. They will not lack anything as long as I am there. They will definitely become part of our family and we*

> shall take care of them together. He added as he held me
> into his hands, hugged me and comforted me.
- *I will think about it my dear. I told him to simply calm his emotions down.*
- *Ok. Thank you. Chérie, make sure you take care of yourself. He simply said.*

The hugs from my fiancé and the smell of his perfume thereof always calmed my spirit. I always wanted to remain in the comfort of his arms. The long conversation that I had with my fiancé was consoling. I knew he was going to be there for me and to help me in my family challenges. By having me as their father, my siblings did not feel orphans anymore, at least not very much. They revealed to me on New Year's Eve as we evaluated our achievements during the soon-to-end-year and as we awaited the dawning of a new year that they were really worried after our father died and wondered how they were going to survive since the five of us were still in school and with no income left by our late father.

- *I really thought it was the end of the world for us. I did not tell you but I despaired. Taking into consideration how my health was fragile, I thought my end was soon coming. I did not see myself continuing high school. My father was the only one to always accompany me to the hospital and to assist me in everything I needed. We were not rich but I did not lack anything when he was there. I always felt secure with his presence. The little one started.*
- *We are really blessed to have you darling Nadina. You have been so wonderful to us. You are more than our sister. You turned our worries into mirage. You are an inspiration to us. You became a wonderful father to us. If I recount my testimony and happiness we will not go to bed. I just want to thank you for what you have been to*

us all. I also thank Mzee in absentia for his unwavering support and his encouragement. We surely miss our dad. But we thought that no one was going to fill the gap his death created. But you showed great character and you are up to the task. Testified another.

- As for me, I do not know what to say. This year has been wonderful. Our unity has really been our strength and weapon. I love every moment of our coming together. When I am at school, although lacking the basics I need, I get a consoling message from one of you asking me not to despair, for we are in this together. I thank Nadina for all her efforts to keep us going and hoping, she is an extraordinary woman. God could not have given us a better sister. We are really blessed to have her around. Blessed is the man who will have her as a wife. Mbanda retorted.

- It is my pleasure my dearest siblings —I almost said children. The only reward I ask you is to do your best in the education that you are currently receiving. This is the moment to plan for a brighter future. The foundation is established now. The future is planned today. I am glad that you are taking seriously your studies. That is the best you can give me in return. And I already have an impression that you are doing your best. I am happy for you. Let us make our parents proud. They are not with us physically but they are in touch with us and follow closely our life journey. Mzee is not able to be with us because of his religious commitment but he is with us in spirit and assures us of his prayers and moral support. He asked me to greet you and to commend your efforts during this last year. I added.

*These occasional gatherings are what keep us together. They create a bond, a unity, and support for one another. We cease the opportunity to evaluate what we achieved and to plan ahead together. The occasions are our secret that the enemy fails to grasp. They are our weapon against tough times. Our unity is like that mustard seed that grew with time to make something great that even ended up convincing those who despised us and became a shelter for them.*

*My siblings have ceased to feel orphans. They are not the only ones not to feel orphans; due to various reasons, I have ceased to feel orphan. Almost automatically, Mzee and Mbanda are not only my brothers but each one of them in their unique ways has also become like a father to me, advising me on a number of issues, and being there for me always as I already told you in my very first email. Mzee calls me each and every week to find out how his little brother and sisters are doing since I promised to act as a bridge. He is really a generous young man who has decided to give his life to God and for the salvation of his fellow humans. Rerwa and Hoza are not just my sisters but they became like my mother; each one in her capacity advising me. I listen to them and always appreciate their ingenious ideas and advice. My observation is that children grow very fast. Recently, I listened to Rerwa thank the parents who hosted her for one year as she was preparing those who were about to sit for their national exams. I was convinced that she had grown and had become wise over the past few years. With all my siblings, we share the burden that life brings upon us, we also share the joys that come our way. Honestly, our burden became lighter once we turned mother and father to each other. Having my siblings as my father and mother made me avoid the spirit of paternalism over them. I gave them the freedom they needed and they responded to me by becoming responsible ladies and young men. I am really proud of them. I am happy to be part of this beautiful family. Your love and example have kept us united and going.*

*Your death was unexpected and that is probably why you never left neither heritage nor testimony. After realising that even the little money I had was used for the funeral, I despaired even more. It was going to be difficult to obtain basic needs. I concluded you had left with me an impossible mission. We thought we were doomed and condemned to live in misery. In fact, we did not know whether there was a family account or not. Certainly there was but we do not know who knew it. We had no doubt that it should be on the same account that the money you received from selling the farms in Ndegeya where we were born and grew up. During the time of laying the tomb stone, people are expected to say whether they owe anything to the deceased or whether they are owed something. They take the opportunity to disclose any important information they have that may help those that are survived by the deceased. Since we were not privileged to get any response from anyone even during the day of laying the tomb stone we decided to think hard about other alternatives. But we knew that some of your friends owed you money but they did not want to pay back. They felt no obligation to pay us since you were no more.*

*How many people steal the money of the deceased when they discover that no one will ever find out that they shared it with or owed it to the deceased? This was a sheer reminder of how people become dishonest because of money and abuse the friendship and trust that they had with those who cross the river. Some even kill to confiscate the money of those they worked with or for. What a selfish world. I wonder what such kind of people will do when they get to meet those they cheated. If only they knew that cheating does not necessarily make their life better let alone making them happier. They always ignore that they will not come to your side with that money as you said in your previous email. Even if they were to come with it, I wonder whether it is of any use in your world. All this behaviour makes me wonder. Do people who wronged each other on earth live together on your side? Do they forget what happened while they were on this side? Do they learn automatically to forgive one another? How free are you by the way in your world? Are these values of freedom, forgiveness, togetherness, love etc used to describe the kind of life you live?*

*When I realised that we were left in such a terrible and poor situation, I decided to use the little money I had on me for the funeral and afterwards. Moreover, I got little money from people during mourning. To that I added little money that I had deposited in an account for four years (10% of my monthly student allowance). I used all that money to rehabilitate the house you used for many years as a carpentry workshop. With that money, I could only afford to change the shape without replacing the old tiles. Out of two rooms it had we managed to make a living room and two rooms, a decent house for a small and poor family in Kayiga. My brother was preparing to go to Rome for studies after being sent by his O Dei superiors to do his masters in Political Science. He was not a burden to me since I did not spend much on him except when I would take a bus to visit him in his community in Kayiga. I regret that I could not afford to treat him to a nice dinner in the most expensive restaurant in Kayiga. But I am consoled that now I can make up for all those lost opportunities.*

*The burden was on how to raise the other three siblings, feed them and keep them in school up to the university level. By rehabilitating the house, I thought that my siblings would get small income for their basic and school needs from leasing that house. So I would not be troubled a lot having had to take care of my children and not annoying my husband with too many requests from my siblings once we get married even if he had acknowledged that they will automatically become part of his family and his responsibility.*

*Because of urbanisation, a number of families have migrated to the city to look for jobs. These families usually do not have their own houses and have no choice but to hire houses to live in.*

*Similarly, a big percentage of those who wed nowadays in the city find it hard to build a new house from scratch and decide to live in other people's houses and pay them little money each month as they gather money that will buy a house later, if at all their salary will allow them to. Many are those who hire houses for the rest of their lives.*

*Still, the newly rehabilitated house took many months to get one person to rent it. Finally, Sam, our relative rented the house. He lived in the house for four months but he only paid for the first two months. When the third month was over Mbanda approached him and asked him why he was not paying. Sam asked him to be patient with him for few days. The fourth month, Mbanda was told the same story. Initially, we were happy that a relative was in the house and was not going to cause a lot of headache as some other tenants do in this city especially if they occupy the house of a poor person with no much authority. Unfortunately now we could not chase him just as we could have done if he was not our relative. We would simply have given him a 20-day notice as the city's policy allows. At the beginning of the fifth month Sam disappeared never to return. Some people knew where he was but he would not come to remove his belongings. We had to remove them to make way for other people who wanted to occupy the house. We could not sell some of Sam's property to get the money he owed us for he was our relative. We begged him to send people to collect his belongings.*

*A number of people came after Sam and have lived in that house kept my siblings going because of the money they pay each month. Currently the house is occupied by someone who is a relative; I am crossing my fingers that he will not end up being like Sam and walk away without completing his payment. But it is unlikely. It has been almost a year and the relative is paying even better than the other landlord. The government taxes however seem too much. Many poor people complain that the government* takes most of what they get and it is as if they work for the government.

The period when we had to wait for someone to rent the house became like a nightmare and was rubbing salt to the yet to heal wound caused by losing you to the other world at such a young age. I almost regretted the initiative of rehabilitating that house and thought I would have offered the money to my siblings to use it as they pleased. At the university, I spent sleepless nights wondering what the children were eating back home. I could neither concentrate in my studies nor at work and I sometimes used that to justify the bad quality of a few of my essays during my studies.

The first few months of my married life were difficult for I kept wondering how tough the situation was at home with my siblings. My husband wondered why I had lost so much weight but I would tell him it was because of my studies combined with stress at work. I would tell him that my boss does not always like what I do because I go against his position that our TV station although private should not criticize what the government is doing no matter how unfair it is. This complaint against my boss at work was true but not enough to put me under such stress as I was having. The reality at work is a sign that the press in our country is not as free as it is supposed to be. Justice and fairness seem not to be the prime motivation of journalists. It is about the government's interests and that of the TV owners who are promised rewards by government officials rather than telling the people the truth. I always try to avoid saying what the government wants but it is not always an easy task. I wonder whether they will keep me for long with such an attitude since I do not do what they want but what I am supposed to do as a professional journalist. I believe we have to dig down and find out what the government does and to push for fair and just policies that would benefit the weak and the poor.

*But what counts? Following media ethics or pleasing the boss and his friends in the government and earning your salary at the end of the month? This is certainly a question that many journalists grapple with and many decide to dance to the tune of their boss lest they get sacked and lose the little privileges they had. But I refuse to buy into that behaviour. I refuse to be coward and to put my interests ahead of the people that I am meant to serve. What is the purpose of the media? We were taught that we are supposed to be the voice of the voiceless groups and to commend those who are doing well and to help those who are derailing come back to rails. What we learnt in school does in no way correspond to what we find on the ground unfortunately. But I will try to be that small light that shines in darkness even if it is to help one person for this small light may enlighten the very person to bring about ways that would enlighten and free his fellow human beings. I chose journalism because I fell in love with it and more so because it was an easy way to help me achieve my goal and dream of eradicating poverty.*

*Many people have been wondering why I had to go back to school since I already finished my degree some time ago. Dear father, things have changed a lot in my country since you left. Many are those women who combine raising their children, working and studying. Many universities in our country contain relatively old people who have gone back to school so that they can compete with others in this age where education has become of great value. If one does not go to school, sooner or later one realises that the job will be taken by someone else who is more qualified. With an unemployment rate high, one has to have a master's degree to make a living and to compete in the search for a job. To get qualified one has no choice but to go back to school while at the same time remaining at the same work. Of course getting a higher degree is no guarantee that the salary will be increased; far from it. It is only a guarantee that no one else will take the job from you. I have been working for five years and my salary is still the same. The danger, however, is that some universities knowing the context of the country offer so many programs but with little substance. Students do not seem to care much either and do not work hard for they look more for the paper —the degree — than the knowledge they acquire. As long as they know that they will pass they relax and focus on other issues. Some even go to the extreme of making their thesis written from other people knowing that they will not have to defend it as it used to be the case before. But I have refused to take the easy road. Knowledge I acquire will help me achieve my dream of fighting poverty and do my job better. It is not about keeping my position from being taken by someone or for the sake of earning higher degree but to improve the quality and the scope of my knowledge. Despite the loophole in education in this country, there are many other students who take education serious as well.*

*What is clear across the nation is that education has now become the only crop worth cultivating after realising that the land is insufficient and will remain so in the years to come with the ever growing population density. Now that the land even belongs to the state, the latter can take it from you anytime without much compensation and hence some people feel it is not secure like it used to be to invest in land especially when one is in the category of the poor. Indeed education has become the only heritage that a parent can give to his descendants since there is no more land to offer in heritage.*

*Some are women who after giving birth decide to quit their job to raise their kids. They do so for one or two years. But I cannot afford to do so. Not only do I need the money to take care of my siblings and my family but also our life expectancy in this country seems short to allow me that luxury. I therefore have to combine school, work, raising my kids and taking care of my siblings. At times, it feels too much and I feel like running crazy. When my husband is not around, I take time to cry and release tension. Although I tell him about hard times that I go through, I do not want to worry him so much and bother him with my tears. But he has been such a gentleman who understands me and supports me so much. He truly has a big and loving heart. I do not feel on my own for he helps me in all those areas. Each time we come back from work, he takes one to two hours taking care of the baby boy. He plays with him, feeds him and now he even knows how to bath him. That allows me to gain some time to do my homework. When it comes to statistics and other mathematical issues my husband also explains to me for he is so good at that domain. He also challenges me in my work and gives me constructive ideas and advice. He has been there for me since your death and assists me in so many ways in raising my siblings. I wonder how I could have managed if he was not around. I thank God for giving me such a wonderful husband. I could not wish for a better person.*

*There is no doubt that the living conditions of my siblings let alone my own family had affected my postgraduate studies. If I used to read 100 pages a day, I was reading 50 and still would not understand it all unlike when I was doing my undergraduate. But I never allowed their problems to interfere with my career for it was the very career that would sometimes put bread on their table when the motorbike had a problem or the landlord had delayed paying.*

*Dear Hachris, do not worry about me because this is how life is on our side of the river as you may have experienced it. But what I have learnt, despite the struggles is that, if I had left money to my siblings instead of rehabilitating the house the money would have finished in a few months and they would be struggling right now. I am sure you realise how much we have achieved in so much little time. It is true that the more money one gets the more the needs become. The months I had to wait to get someone to lease the house taught me that patience is a virtue and it pays to be patient. Now the house is still there and being leased to various people and we have even managed to replace old tiles with new ones. The previous tiles had given us a lot of headache because the house would leak most of the times in the rain season and Mbanda would be under pressure to work on it to treat customers in a good manner. A number of landlords had to leave the house because it was leaking. Because we used the little money we get from the house to rehabilitate it, it took us some time to fix that problem of tiles.*

*Initially I had asked our stepmother, Don, to keep 50% of the money we got from leasing the house each month for renovating other parts and for some school needs of my siblings but she always found the money insufficient even for food. This may have been right especially with life in Kayiga city having become more expensive over the years and currently the most expensive capital city in the region. But it may also be because of what I just said that when one gets money, one also gets competing needs on which to spend the money. It is also similar to what you said in your previous email that money is never enough, that humans are never satisfied. Although the money we get from the house is very little, it helps in children's upkeep including buying food and paying their maid for twenty days. I cover the remaining ten days. But if I am to accomplish the role of a father I have to be more present in their lives than just giving them part of my salary every month. That is why I talk to one of them every day to find out how they are doing. On some weekends and each time I get a break and go to visit them, I realise that they are living a decent life and do not complain much in this city where many people are struggling to eat twice let alone three times a day. Even some of those who eat twice cook once and have to warm the rest in order to save charcoal or electricity.*

*Truly my siblings and I have come a long way. Despite challenges here and there that can make me cry I realise that they are living far better than they were in the recent past. The fact that my siblings can get the basic items has now become a consolation to me and has boosted my morale in my studies and my family life. My husband asks me why I have become happier after some years of struggle and I refer him to the happiness of my siblings as partly the cause of my happiness. I suppose he was right I should not have worried to much as I did. But maybe it is because I was worried that I exactly became determined and was able to set up measures to take care of my siblings. I am aware that there are many children who are head of families in this country especially after the war that ravaged our motherland and I will not rest until they get the right treatment. As a journalist, I have to play advocacy role. I need to let people know that it is not simply having a lot that makes one happy but knowing how to share the little one has with those that do not have anything; those who are not happy. When I am done with my studies I will have to do more than advocating for these orphaned children. I am not sure what kind of service I should render to them but I will have to find something to do to make their lives a lot more bearable.*

*Dear Hachris, I thank you for inspiring in me that idea of rehabilitating and leasing the house and inspiring in Mbanda the idea of buying a motorbike. I believe in the ancestors' contribution and power over the living. I have no doubt now that you heard my request on the day you passed on to the land of the living dead. I did not cry in vain when I remained at the tomb requesting your unwavering support. You have put to shame our enemies. There is no doubt that the tough words you told your Leader once you reached where you are living now had an impact. He may not have responded but if truly your Leader possesses all the powers we believe Him to have there is no way He was going to let us down.*

*I know when you were still alive you never wanted anyone to come and share the same compound with us let alone leasing our house indefinitely because you always cherished privacy and peace in our home. Our space was sacred and it wasn't supposed to be invaded by strangers let alone those who would live there for a long time.*

*Of course now things have changed, you are no longer there to labour for us and so we had to do it the hard way. It seems to be working well though. In as much as I value privacy and peace, I want to beat poverty. I want to provide a decent life to my siblings. But do not worry many are the families that lease their houses nowadays especially in Kayiga to beat the expensive bills of water and electricity, to pay school fees for their children, to afford medical care and to beat food prices that keep rising. Some people even lease their main house only to live in cottages. Last month there was a couple that came from Europe to get married. For a whole month, they lived in a house whose owners live in the cottage. Such kind of business is growing.*

*Although education has become the only heritage to give to one's son, it does not necessarily guarantee employment in this nation. Many of my schoolmates have been waiting for three years without employment when they thought their misery was going to be over. I hope Mbanda will not take long to get employment so that he can take up the burden that I have been carrying of supporting two families. It doesn't get any easier but I am ever resilient and hopeful. I never thought a woman could accomplish all that I am doing. But I am sure you taught me how to be a good father. I have come to realise that I did not have to be a man to accomplish your role of father. Those who mocked me when I stayed on the grave to plead with you got it totally wrong. Now they are quiet though and know in their heart that I am not just doing it but I am doing it very well. Some people tease me that I am two in one. But I wonder why this should be said only when a woman is concerned. There is no doubt that it is how our patriarchal society has made us to think. I am sure it will change slowly.*

*I dream of a society where inequality will cease to dictate the rules of the game. I dream of a society where all children will have their rights fulfilled and in which the poor will be taken care of and women fully respected for who and what they are. I dream of a society where the orphan will no longer be sidelined and left to suffer and die in poverty. I dream of a society where those who have will cease to exploit the have-nots to increase their having and where being will be the order of the day and will help us to carry each other along. I dream of a nation in which women will be represented in decision making institutions. I dream of a society where women who die while giving birth will dramatically reduce. I dream of a society where children will never die young. I dream of a society where a boy child will never be preferred to a girl child when it comes to education. I dream of a society in which the poor will not be marginalised. I dream of a society where every person will be free to air their views and to live secure. I dream of a society where no person will be marginalised because of their skin colour. I dream of a world of peace where guns will keep quiet and where terrorists will become a history. We do not really want any kids to suffer the way we have suffered. We do not want any more kids to be orphaned by wars and conflicts organised by some people to get power and money. These people do not seem to think about others but are only blinded by their interests and gains.*

*Dear father, pray your master so that he intervenes and turn our selfishness and hatred into love. Dear father I hope I do not tire you with long emails but it is important that you know how far we have come. I do not know how time is managed at your side.*

# My destiny, my freedom, my happiness

The reply Nadina got from her father was very educative and informative. It reminded her of how he was when she was young. He used to gather them together so that they receive advice from him. He would tell them to work hard and get prepared for life out there if they want to be important people who could make change to the world, the change that the world was craving for. He was barely educated but the wise words that came out of his mouth showed how talented and unique he was. People often said that he is naturally intelligent and a wise man. This sort of gathering was always a moment that every child at home would long for. They learnt that many people will always remember him for the way he counselled them and advised them.

*Dear Nadina, I am glad to hear that you and your siblings have grown in responsibility and wisdom and that you are taking care of siblings very well despite your other responsibility in your family with your child and your husband and your work. Thank your husband on my behalf. I guess he is a nice husband to you; a good model to many couples in that country. I am really impressed by the way you have grown in wisdom and insight and the way you have great dreams. I wish you all the best as you work hard for your other dreams to come true. I will play my part so that you achieve what you desire to make the world better, more just and safer for the orphan, the weak and the poor. Maybe you are right that my strong words to our Leader has interceded on your behalf and made some impact. Keep telling me about your country so that I could go back to Him to request assistance to that country that I miss so much but that I would love to hear that it has transformed into a peaceful, prosperous and united country.*

*Shame that I never got to attend your wedding and see my in-law nor my grand-children but that is destiny and I could not have changed anything. No one will escape their destiny however free they are, no matter how rich and powerful they are. All things said, I do not regret being here. I am happy here. I am finally at home where death will no longer have any impact on me, where I do not have to worry anymore that I will grow old, where there is no conflict and no hatred. I did not run away from responsibility as you know. I would never do that. All I ask of you is not just to follow my example but to be where I could not be, to do what I could not do, to succeed where I have failed and to do better where I did good, to fight where I relaxed, to excel where I was ordinary, to run where I walked, to speak out where I kept quiet but also to keep quiet where I needlessly spoke out. Make sure you instil these values in your siblings. Most of these things are never taught at school.*

*Be always ready for the unknown and the surprises. I always trusted in your wisdom and insight. I always admired how you worked very hard at school and felt I was one of the few blessed parents to have you as my daughter. I was 90 % sure that you would always top the class and even beat boys. You never proved me wrong. Guess what, I almost preferred Mzee to you when I debated on who to send to school. The reason was no other than* the fact that that time girls were not taken to school simply because their fathers always thought that their daughters take the money they earn at work to the family where they get married. But a boy child is always the head of the family and so was expected to assist his parents even after he had formed his own family. How men of our time were selfish and ignorant! Thank fate I never fell in that trap and that kind of old-fashioned patriarchal thinking. The truth is not that parents lack money to pay for education of their children but inspired by a patriarchal way of thinking they become selfish and rather than thinking about the good of their kids they think about their own good and become obsessed on how they will live in their old age. They sacrifice the life of a girl child as they waste the money that was meant for the girl child education. I decided to quit beer for three years in order to take both of you to school. Now I realised that had I heeded the behaviour of selfish men in patriarchal society, your siblings would be suffering. The world would be lacking your aptitudes and capabilities. Do not be surprised when people in that society doubt the capability of women. That is exactly how we were raised up to believe. But it is up to you and your fellow women to change that mentality. I am glad that you are already working hard to prove our society wrong. It will take some time but I am convinced that you will get there one day. You will one day be hailed as the women's freedom and rights fighter.

The other thing I always admired about you Nadina is that for you it was not just about getting good grades but also good character because without both, education is incomplete. How many intelligent people have made the world lag behind? How many of wars in Africa are caused by those we call intelligent? How many people have more than one doctoral degree but still fail to see the injustices that take place around them because of selfishness? Some of them commit the very injustices. How many people used their education to exploit resources on our continent?

*How many educated people we have in position of leadership but cannot devise ways of exploiting natural resources? They only content themselves of dirty money they receive in the exchange of giving a market to corrupt people from other countries and continents. Intelligence without character has made people exploit and exterminate others. It has made leaders sell out their nations to foreigners and betray their fellow countrymen. Intelligence without character and moral values and principles have made people become selfish; have misled them in their quest for happiness and thirst for power. If intelligence and good character were always emphasised in our children's education the world will be a better place now. Those with intelligence but no character fail to understand that happiness is not about having a lot of money and big material things but happiness comes from within because you are just satisfied with what you are and who you are. The ultimate happiness, the chief good, the final goal, the Summum Bonum, as we say here may not be achieved while still on earth but it is an ideal that is worth following every morning of your days on earth. The closer we work to achieve it the happier we become, the better our life turns. Justice and fairness amount to allowing fellow human beings to achieve happiness as long as they obey laws in their quest of happiness. Some of our leaders lack intelligence while others lack character. In some worse scenarios, some leaders lack both intelligence and character. All these at different degrees exploit their people rather than assisting them. They indulge in corruption and injustice and amassing assets that they rush to keep in democratic industrialised countries.*

*When the journey on earth is complete you will be able to let go the little you possess as you painfully cross the river to embrace that ultimate happiness. However, possessing assets in itself is not a bad thing as long as one did neither steal these assets nor exploit the weak and the poor to get them. The unfortunate thing is that only few people know how to use their riches wisely. If one has things these should help one to move close to that ideal rather than taking one away from the ideal like it happens to many people. Many are those who are rich but not happy, have big houses but shelter-less, have big beds but cannot sleep, enough food but no appetite, body guards but no security and peace of mind, much power and yet powerless, freedom but no free will, are intelligent but not wise. Use what you have wisely and be satisfied and you will be happy. Daughter, be happy. Help your siblings and your children to be happy as well. Help the nation and the whole world through your career to take interest in fellow humans' interests. Many are those who have things and keep wanting to get more and as a result they, in the process, exploit the poor. Denounce that selfish attitude.*

*P.S. I was very much consoled when I got here for I met with former members of our basketball team, Opika: Muza, Muvu, Ruta, etc., our former neighbours in Ndegeya: Sam, Bito, Bwe, Ndu, etc. and my father and mother and other relatives. What a reunion! My kind regards to all those who knew us. Our thoughts are always with you. We wish you well.*

*Your father, Hachris*

# A generation of killers

The more Nadina writes emails to her father, the more she misses him and the more she thinks of her mother and her past memories quickly and suddenly come to life. She relives the past with its painful scenarios. "Who do you love the most between me and your father?" she remembers the question her mother once asking her. That was and is still a hard question. Nadina did not care whom she loved the most; the essential thing was that she loved both of them and still loves her father and her mother.

Now that both of her father and mother are gone she even loves them more. The more she misses her father and mother the more she loves them. She believes they still love her too. Indeed she still feels their love supporting and guiding her in the harsh times of the world and as she takes care of her siblings and plays the role of a father towards her siblings. It is indeed the very love that has made her become who she is. The love she received bore fruits and has expanded not just to her siblings but to other people. There are so many brothers and sisters who do not assist each other. Some even prefer to assist other members of the largest family and other strangers.

It is another day, and Nadina decides to go back to her meditation routine lest she gets addicted to this email business and forgets her God, the Almighty who creates her daily and sustains her all the time. But still in her meditation she cannot stop thinking of her mother and reliving the past. Although she had a very special relation with her father she also got along well with her mother. But probably because the mother left for the other world so early the bond between the two was shaken.

Nadina finds it really unfortunate that as children they never got to know the fate of their mother. They lost touch with her on the worst Sunday of the most cruel month and year of their country's history while they were running away from the war zone. Later on they learnt that rebels had taken control of Kayiga International airport. During today's meditation she cannot run away from some ideas. She remembers very well how much money her father had to pay to various soldiers who threatened to kill them. She always contemplates how most of her aunts and uncles perished during that dark period of our history. She has failed to understand how people can massacre people with whom they share more or less the same culture, neighbourhood and nation. What madness entered these people who dared kill their brothers and sisters? She cannot find answers and she is yet to find someone who has discovered why. Perhaps Shakespeare had a point: "the near in blood, the nearer bloody." But Nadina wonders why not just her people but people in general should work hard to prove Shakespeare right. She remembers a colleague from another country who said that to calm down the mad soldiers and militias who were killing people during the genocide against Tutsi, this colleague's father would always appeal to his friends who were soldiers so that killers could spare her mother during the war. Nadina hopes that after two disastrous wars that took the lives of her parents within a space of two decades there will never be another one. Although the country is becoming more peaceful, there are still wars and conflicts in some neighbouring nations and other African nations. Next month she will interview a rebel movement in the neighbouring country to learn about motives of guerrillas. She hopes to make a documentary out of that field research. Her intention is to make the world aware of destructive nature of wars and conflicts to the society.

She wonders whether it is because of money that some of her beloved ones survived or it was their destiny. No one would ever find out. There are many people who had much more money than my father but they ended up being killed. Some killers were so mad that nothing could stop them from carrying out their evil behaviours. Due to this continuous payment of money, Nadina's family was left with no money and her father had to borrow from a neighbour so that they can survive in that terrible period —which she wishes had never been part of their history. She wonders what would have happened if those evil soldiers had come to request for more money. Luckily, they did not come back. She fights tears on her chick as she recalls part of the testimony she once gave during a conference on International Conflicts:

"...As the war advanced on us we could no longer bear the bullets falling in our compound or piercing our tiles and falling inside our house. The sound of bombs had become natural to our ears. How lucky we were that those bombs fell on farms near us and never on our house. I remember each day when we were going to fetch water and firewood during the war, we would discover new holes in people's farms and sometimes on the side of the road created by bombs —so were we told —that failed to explode. I wondered whether they would explode in the future killing innocent people who did not have anything to do with the war. It was very easy to hear a whole family that was decimated by bombs. In fact, as we went to fetch water and fire wood, we could see houses completely destroyed by these bombs and those we asked said that no one survived in that house. Many years have passed by since the war came to an end. But no one seems to care about telling effects that these bombs and bullets have had on our lives and the lives of our kids. Many kids are dying of cancer and all sorts of illness that we never experienced before the war. Studies should be conducted to find out whether these new illnesses that take the lives of our innocent children are related to guns or whether these illnesses existed before but our medical system could not detect them since it was not well developed.

Although war is over in my country, wars are still rampant in many countries and there are so many hands behind those wars and conflicts. Dear people who are attending this conference and who are from democratic industrialised countries tell your leaders that we need peace. They are the ones who illegally sell arms to rebel movements and by so doing allow people to exterminate one another. We do not manufacture weapons in my country. But because some African countries have so many natural resources they have become a battleground for powerful nations, each wanting to get a bigger share. This has torn the African continent apart and has left it very poor. When will the heart of humans change and yield to peace? When will we learn to take interest in other people's interest rather than determining everything according to our interests? When will we learn to respect our fellow human beings' rights? When will we live in a fair and just world? When will powerful nations be held accountable for their irresponsible behaviour in weak nations?

When the fighting intensified we decided to leave our house. Like the biblical Abraham, we did not know where we were going we only trusted in God, as we crossed ways with bullets and soldiers whose identity we ignored. The night became like the day being lightened by unstoppable fires of bullets. Having grown up near a military camp where we heard bullets everyday from soldiers' training, we found it normal hearing the sound of guns. But this time around we knew that circumstances had changed especially with night gun shots. Even kids could neither afford to sleep nor to get hungry. That very night we got caught up in the fighting, and got scattered through the shootings. It took some days to find each other many miles away from where the fighting had caught us up–I remember we reconnected with my sister Rerwa when we reached another city a week later. We thought she had passed away. Many are those who lived their last night on that cursed day. We had to jump their dead bodies and we became traumatised at those scenes that we never experienced before. From that day arose in me another dream of making and fighting for peace. For now I am not really sure of what to do and how to do it. But this talk in this conference is just a beginning. I am a simple journalist in our nation and for there to be peace there is need for transnational and intergovernmental cooperation. It is not easy to be heard and to make impact on the international stage.

Since we did not know about circumstances surrounding the death of our mother, we always hoped to get reconnected to our mother but that was never going to happen. Decades later, we are still ignorant of the circumstances over her death. Money was just a delaying tactic and a way of cheating death. But can we really cheat death? Many are those children on our continent who suffer the same fate of not knowing what befell their parents because of so many wars and conflicts. Many are those parents who lost their beloved children to a war that befell on them. Some even never got the chance to bury their kids. Others are still traumatised for having buried their own children with no assistance from others.

But what really happened to our mother? We always asked our father. Apparently, the following day after we left home, our mother was shot dead together with the last born, a one-year-old girl, Nti. Nti is definitely a saint and is interceding for us. We had no ways of verifying that incident of our mother's death. Neither did our father. That is why the following two years, like many people, he kept writing messages to relatives, through, Red Cross and other Non-Governmental Organisations, asking them our mother's whereabouts and fate. We always believed that she went missing but not dead and that we would see her somewhere one day. In all those countries I have travelled I always entertained the possibility of meeting my mother thinking that she may have fled into a foreign land. But if she really had would she not have contacted us? During five years that followed the war, I dreamt a reunion with her, seeing her cooking the good fish for us again, taking us to church and to the market to buy us new clothes and shoes. Even today, at my age I once in a while dream about that reunion. What joy will that have been! What joy will it be when we meet again face to face and embrace her once more in the bliss of heaven. Will there really be such a moment as believers imagine? It is not very important for this conference but in my country, we have just discovered a way of communicating with those who departed this world before us. I have had very enlightening exchange of emails with my father that I intend to share with the world in the years to come. I am aware that in this nation where the conference is held just like many other advanced countries people no longer believe in life after this world.

During the war, our mother sensed the bloody death coming. She always told us that

- I have survived the death in the hands of the killers who massacred my people in previous wars but I wonder whether I will survive the war this time around.

- Mother, do not worry. Only God is our protector, I remember telling her.

She never survived that war. May her soul rest in eternal peace! I always wondered who I should blame for the death of my mother. How can I forgive that person if I find out who it is? Woe to those who fuel wars and turn happy children into orphans. But who can I really blame? The fighters? The killers? The leaders? Those who planned the bloody conflict? Those who gave birth to my mother? The sponsors of wars? Gun manufacturers? God? Fate? Those who sell guns to our continent? Those who divide us for their own interests? All of these? Who can I really judge? Who can I acquit? Where is our mother's body buried? We may not know where her body is or was but we always believe that her soul is somewhere being rewarded for the wonderful care she gave us. Each time I think of my mother and the fate she suffered I cry. Sometimes my husband finds me crying and wonders why. Maybe he thinks that women like crying.

Crying is one of the few ways I can release tension and come to terms with what happened, at least for a while. I pity some men who never cry for those they loved."

When Nadina came from the conference she had one day off. The following day, she went to work. She came back early that day because there was no much news to report and she was still feeling tired from the journey because she is not as used to travelling as her husband. She took a shower and put on a white dress. She combed her long and elegant hair. She went to the veranda to enjoy the breeze and the setting of the sun. She got inspired to write her father an email that he would deliver to her mother. As she thought about her mother, a tear fell from her cheek. Her energy seemed to run away from her. The thought of communicating with her mother was an opportunity for Nadina to tell her how much she has missed her care and love and that life at times felt meaningless without her. Nadina went to her room, took a computer, brought it to the veranda and started writing.

# Dear Mum

As I cry again in honour of my mother, dear Hachris, I enclose a message for my mother:

*Oh mother, wherever you are, I have a feeling that you are happy and are still beautiful like before. I remember your beautiful smile, a smile that you contaminated to me. People never believed that we were your children. Less would they have believed it now were you still alive! Were you still alive, they could not believe that Hachris junior and Dativa —my son and daughter whom I decided to name after my father and my mother respectively – are your grandchildren. Even yourself, you were always in owe to see us as your children for you regarded yourself too young to give birth to all of us. Indeed, under your care, generosity and protection, we were growing very fast. Each time we went to visit our grandmother you looked at us and were amazed at how fast we had grown and you would always murmur to my grandmother "will I really be able to raise these children of mine?" You were well aware of wars and conflicts that had torn apart our nation for decades. You hardly experienced moments of peace in your life. My grandmother would assure you that you are such a courageous and devout lady that you would manage to raise your kids.*

*Yes you did raise us even if destiny took you before you accomplished what you desired and had done so well. But do not worry we have now grown up into responsible ladies and men; we are your pride and you live in us. As you probably have seen in some of the emails I have written to my father and as you shall read in others, myself and my siblings, your children, are doing very well. Recently, I wrote to Hoza and asked her how life was treating them and she said:*

- *Life is treating us well, even if it gets tough here and there, we are grateful for the sacrifices you, as our sister, unceasingly make so that our life gets better each day. We are really blessed to have you as our sister. We are as ever united and we do things together for the wellbeing of our family. Unity and love have been the pillars of family and our secret to survive the challenges of Kayiga city. The love that we sucked from our mother's breast and the love our parents showered upon us in the short period that we lived with them has been our shield and our protector. Dear sister, we wish you to found your family on love.*

*I keep encouraging siblings and agree with Hoza that life has its challenges but we have to learn to move forward in those challenges as you taught us. Together we shall overcome the difficulties. When those people who know you meet us, they quarrel about whether or not we are your children for we have grown so fast in proportion to our age. I write this email specifically to tell you that you should no longer be worried: God loves orphans. He is their father and mother par excellence. I simply help him to do so. This goodness and love of God, I realised and learnt through the tough task I had of raising my siblings. And indeed I am a witness to that love of God towards orphans. On my behalf and on behalf of my siblings, I wish to tell you that we love you and we miss you so much. Thank you for having carried each of us for nine months and for the pain you underwent to educate us. Nine months times six. You left this world with Nti our last born. She was so young for us to even remember how she looked like. After giving birth to two children and having realised how painful it is, I even learnt to appreciate you for I became well aware of how much you suffered for our sake. You went on to raise us like no other mother raised her kids. I bet if there were prizes of "mother of the month" you would have scooped most of them. Thank dad on our behalf for he accomplished the role of father and mother when you had departed from us. This heritage of love you bestowed on us we will hand it on to our kids hoping that they will also pass it on generations to come. As such you have greatly contributed to the peace we enjoy today and we shall enjoy tomorrow. The little effort that each one of us does has a long lasting impact on the rest of the society. Similarly, the evil that some people have done has destroyed our country and made it lag behind in many areas.*

*Thank you for having been a good and loving mother, for having taken good care of us, care we have been missing for two decades now. Teach me to follow in your footsteps as I raise my children —your grandchildren —and my siblings —your children. Teach me to be gentle. Teach me to endure the harshness of our world. Teach me to be humble. Teach me to care more for fellow human beings. Teach me love. Your love is our shield and our example. Your generosity is a mirror that we use to see whether we resemble you. Your care is a measure that we adopted to take care of those who suffer and toil daily in this world of ours. Teach today's mothers to care for their children. Teach some of those parents that seem not to care about their children and those who, because of poverty, give up their children and take their children's lives and at times their very own lives ignoring that life is a gift from God. Our love to you keeps growing stronger. Out of sight is not out of mind. We will always love you and cherish your generosity upon us. We shall forever cherish good times we spent together when we were kids.*

*Dear mum, please if you can kindly open an email account so that in the future I would be able to talk to you directly like we used to when we were kids. I would rather make you an intermediary if I want to talk to my father rather than making my father a medium when I want to talk you. We look forward to getting reunited again. That will be the happiest day ever of our life. On my behalf, on behalf of my siblings, thank you times a million.*

*Kind regards from your children.*

*Your daughter,*
*Nadina.*

# If one knew

Once in a while, Nadina's father tells her about her mother and the good things she did to the family in particular and the country in general. She was a simple and humble teacher in a small school in her locality. Some of those who passed through her hands went on to become ministers in different governments and others occupy high positions in different domains where they take important decisions that affect the whole nation. Last month she won a posthumous prize of the best teacher of our generation. Even on the other side, she remains a loving mother. She has already forgiven her killers even though she does not really know who they are. Nadina looks forward to receiving her mother's email. That would be one of the best days of her life. She feels that she has now rested and recharged her batteries after a much tasking international conference. While she was thinking of reading Achebe's *Things Fall Apart,* she hears a sound of a received email on her computer. She is convinced that it cannot as yet be a reply of her mother. Although they may have and use time in a way that is different from ours there is no way she could just have finished reading her email and composing another one in a matter of seconds. But still she opens her email fast and realises that it is her father.

*Dear daughter,*

*I hope this email finds you and your family well. Here we are doing fine. I was very glad to see your mother —my wife — once again after more than fifteen years of separation by the bloody war that ravaged our nation. I felt born again and went straight to our Leader to thank Him for that moment of bliss and reunion. On my way to here, I was of course very sad to leave you and especially to go without seeing mon fils Mzee again since he was abroad. I was devastated to pass on to the other world without giving my heritage to you guys. I love you so much that I never expected to leave you so soon.*

*If one knew when death would strike one would be always prepared for it. But unfortunately no one is certain about the hour for it is just a matter of seconds for one to cease being part of one world and to be called to another world. If one knew that one is departing, one would have chance to call one's own to come and bid farewell. You see a journalist on television, and tomorrow you hear he is dead. You wish good night to your neighbour only to wake up without him on your earth. We can really never know about death. In countries that are as insecure as yours death is more common and unpredictable than in other nations.*

*Even more if one knew that where we are going is as good as I have found it, one would console those remaining in the world. Those parties held after a loved one has passed away could then be done while one is still alive to celebrate the departure more or less like people celebrate with their children, say, who are about to go abroad for studies. But this could only be done if one knew when death would strike. Most of the times people have no idea. No matter how painful conditions one may be in, one will be consoled and console others that one is just going to be transformed and at last forever happy.*

*Similarly, those societies that spend a lot of money on celebrating the departure of their loved ones would use the* very money for progress of those who remain behind. I found it outrageous to hear that in some societies they have to wait until they raise enough money for the funeral. Some families in these societies remain in poverty or even in worse condition after the fancy burial for the person who has passed beyond your world. It is time for people to change their behaviour and mentality towards those who pass to the other world. I am sure as a journalist you will work hard for that change in some societies.

I am glad that now there is regular communication between you and myself, between the world and beyond. I hope there will be a change of mind and attitude on your side. It is embarrassing how expensive funerals have become in many parts of the world. It is not fair for so many families who lack the means to bury their own and they find themselves getting loans from the bank to bury their own. Things even become more difficult if the dead has been admitted to the hospital for many months. These families usually spend the little money they have on the sick person and when the latter dies they find that they are unable to pay for the funeral. If you people knew where we have come you would make funerals very simple.

I feel happy here as I told you before. If I knew when I was to come to this side of the world, I would have made sure that you do not struggle as you have struggled. I hope you would forgive me for my not being always ready for the unknown. That is part of human nature. We are limited beings. Of course the eternal joy has incorporated and taken away that sadness I had before coming here. Crossing the river was the most painful experience of my life there. There is no doubt that the love I have for all of you is greater than the shortcomings I had while on earth. No human being is perfect as you would know. By acknowledging one's imperfection, one perfects oneself. The problem that is on earth is that most leaders do not accept when they are at fault. They keep justifying their mistakes and by so doing worsen situations and create more rebellion and hence cause wars.

*Your mother could not believe when she saw me. She shed tears of joy. What showed me how much she still loves you and cares for you is that she asked me whether children had grown up enough to take care of themselves and hence for me to leave them behind. She still loved me and was looking forward to seeing me again but not so soon for she thought my task of raising children was not over yet. I told her confidently that Mzee and Nadina had grown and were therefore in a good position to take care of their brothers and sisters and hence there was no need for her to despair. I wanted her not to despair. I knew it was going to be tough for you Nadina but I knew you would still manage knowing your courage, love and commitment. I assured your mother that even if life wasn't going to be any easy I trust that you will make it. Besides, she knows that it was not my will to leave you behind so prematurely. It is good to realise that your mother looks happy here as well. In fact she has become more consoled and fulfilled since my arrival, so she asserts. So am I. Although there is nothing that lacks here she confessed that she felt incomplete here without me. I am sure I could have felt the same, had I come before her.*

*I have been showing your mother all the emails that you have been writing to me. That consoles her even more. Initially, she could not believe it for she thought she was hallucinating. She has an appointment with our Leader in a few days' time. Once in a while our Leader gets to meet with each one of us to find out how we are doing and whether there is anything that we wish. If there is anything urgent one can make a special appointment and meet the Leader. Your mother wants to take this opportunity to thank Him for all the good things He has done to you —her children; and I quickly added: and our grandchildren. She misses and loves you even more. She would have loved to reply your email but she wants to wait until her meeting with the Leader so that she could incorporate some of the things they will have talked about. She would love to see all of you once again for her consolation to be* complete but she reckons you have to finish your journey on earth first and make sure everyone does their responsibility well. Bloom where you are planted, she seems to suggest and she wishes you every happiness that any good mother would wish her children.

She has taken on the role of a teacher once again. When I told her that she was awarded by the president of your country the best teacher award of the last generation she was not moved very much. I guess it is because of her humility. She said that it was her role and duty to be a good teacher she did nothing special. Since here we do not need those subjects she was teaching she teaches music. People claim that since she took over that position a lot of changes have taken place and the group of singers performs very well. It is like hearing angels sing.

She always prays for a secure and peaceful country. She hopes and prays that your country never see war and ethnic conflict again. She does not want anyone to suffer her fate again. She prays for a genuine reconciliation for all people of all backgrounds in that country. She hopes you campaign for a non-violent, free, just and fair society. She prays and wishes that no politicians put their interests ahead of common people's interests. She always desires that people in any nation be united. "It is very unfortunate that we could not live together as brothers and sisters peacefully", she likes saying.

If all of us knew that we were created in the image of God and are called to co-exist peacefully. Definitely, no one would want to see what befell that beautiful country happening anywhere in the world. No innocent people should be allowed to suffer as we did. Amazingly, she has already forgiven her killers. She asks that you be an instrument of peace, reconciliation and unity in that nation where people seem to remain divided. I wish you joy, peace and happiness. Pass my regards to my children and my grandchildren. I love you all. Looking forward to hearing from you.

Loving dad.

# Determined to liberate

～•～

Nadina has now become accustomed to communicating through email with her father who is on the other side. She wonders whether anyone else in her country has discovered this technology and communication besides her husband –who is still sceptical about the authenticity. She wonders whether others from the other side have been able to take advantage of the same technology to communicate with their loved ones on this side of the world. Taking into consideration that Nadina is a journalist, it would have been easy to spread the news. But their work ethics demands that they spread news for which they have authentic information, that is, information that can be proven in tangible ways. For the time being it is hard to see how it could be justified that she has been talking to her father and her father has been talking to her. It would not be enough to show series of email that they sent to each other. More proofs would be needed. But what proofs? In the meantime Nadina can only enjoy this communication in which she seems to be a pioneer. Now that she has told her father about her brother, she believes it is time to tell him about all other siblings. Today is a holiday, it is a quiet day. There are few cars on the road and that makes the neighbourhood even quieter. One can only hear the gentle sound of rain fall on the tiles. She decides to write her father another message. She decides to begin with Rerwa, her younger sister who comes after Mbanda.

*Dear father, you cannot believe it but Rerwa is a university student. I don't know how but she is. Sometimes, because of not knowing where school fees will come from, I despair and wonder whether she will finish but I believe what made her start will make her finish and we will celebrate her achievements one day. I have come to realise that a number of children in our country do not go to school not that they lack the intellectual aptitudes that it takes but because of the economic constraints which do not allow it. How many children in the villages were clever at school but never got the chance of a government scholarship and had they got it would have finished and got good jobs? They are now condemned to cultivate the rich people's farms to make mincemeat when they were at least supposed to be working in these rich people's offices. Due to these economic constraints and at times negligence of some parents their dreams were shuttered. My work colleague reiterated recently that the number of these children is going to increase since the government has decided to drastically reduce scholarships since it can no longer afford to support as many students as it was able to support in the past. This is due to the fact that Western powers have reduced or cut their aid to our country. Of course this makes me wonder when our nation will become economically independent and acquire a middle income status as my next TV documentary will investigate next week. However, it would be to turn a blind eye not to thank our government for the efforts it put in educating children including Mbanda.*

*Before Rerwa got to the university we never thought she would finish high school for we wondered how she would get money to pay her school fees. Remember, in the recent past the slogan was: no government scholarship no university education for children from poor families. Unlike myself, Mzee and Mbanda, Rerwa never got a scholarship. As time moved, scholarships in our country became restricted to a select few who would have excelled and from poor families. It was hard to imagine that Rerwa would excel since she wrote her exams only few weeks after your death –the death that seriously traumatised her as she loved you so much and was far younger than ourselves. We actually feared she would fail her exams having been affected by your sudden death. Luckily, she passed. Not having a scholarship and not having money to take her in a private university entailed that she would be idle for quite a long period. That is no good for children as you know. When it comes to girl child, idleness is even worse as many cases from our neighbours have demonstrated. A number of our friends and girls from our locality find themselves with unwanted pregnancy. Some of their parents feeling embarrassed they become accomplice of abortion. If they are very unlucky they may lose their daughter. I wanted to protect Rerwa from all these difficulties. I wanted also to reward her courage with which she took the exams.*

*I asked her to think of a simple business project to do to make herself busy and probably to make some money that would help her in her basic needs, and who knows, eventually pay her university tuition fees. After discussing with my husband, I gave her 500 US dollars, the equivalent of my monthly salary. She was not sure what to do for a beginning. She went to the north of the country where she hoped she could make something happen. She put up a coffee, tea, milk and buns shop for people in the village. She quickly realised that village people don't have money for that kind of luxury. They better drink sorghum beer or banana beer for it was cheaper and that is indeed what they were used to. As a consequence Rerwa's project died instantly and she registered a small loss. She confided in me that she was very much disappointed.*

*But I was happy that she made that experience because now outside boarding school, she realised that life was not easy; she learnt that she has to make mincemeat out of difficult situation she was in. She quickly realised that to make any progress requires patience in a country where there are no jobs for a high school graduate and the least one could do is to create one's own job; but even then with the risk of failing —as Rerwa's example proves. In the recent past the government has encouraged the youth to be visionary and innovative enough so as to create their own jobs. This is because finding a job has become so challenging. In fact, she could not even have obtained the cooking job that Mbanda obtained despite being female for now even university students do that kind of job. The self-creation of jobs advocated by the government seems to beg the question. How can one create one's own job when one was not taught how to do it while at school or when one has no money to invest? All that teachers do is to teach students theories. All that the government seems to do is to refer you to banks. All that banks do is to ask you to give a mortgage that you do not even have. Our banks' interest rates are not even encouraging for they are far higher than in neighbouring countries.*

*After the first experience of failure and disappointment that followed, Rerwa did not despair though. I encouraged her to remain patient and to be open to any opportunity that might present itself. Later, she was asked to tutor students who were revising for their national exams. At least she would get some money from their parents to keep her going, to change her hair, to buy lotion. In the meantime I asked her to give me back the money remaining from the failed business project so that I put it on my siblings account for any need that may arise. Moreover, I took the money for fear she could lose it to robbery.*

*Later Rerwa got a part-time job in national land census for a few months. There at least the salary was more than the previous job. When the job was over, she got a half of her salary and was promised to be given the rest later by her boss, Mugabo —a man who was the supervisor of their job. The latter told her that there were other jobs if she liked. Unfortunately, the condition was that she would sleep with him. When she told me that she refused that terrible condition, I was happy for her. Unfortunately, there are a number of girls who are sacrificed on the altar of the material and have to sacrifice their bodies to get jobs in this country. I bet this does not only take place in Mugabo's department but in many more. I am yet to conduct an investigation and later release a documentary on the exploitation of women in our country's administration.*

- *Mugabo is famous in using job tactics to attract girls and in the end sleep with them. How could married men really behave almost like animals and fail to control their libido? Don't they really realise that they are disgracing themselves and their wives? She asked me.*
- *It is very sad that some men could behave like that. Unfortunately, very few girls are like you who prefer integrity, self-respect and poverty to prostitution and self-disrespect. I answered.*
- *When I realised what he wanted I quickly left his office and told him that I am no longer interested in his job. He felt embarrassed and told me that I should not be shy that the job is secured for me.*
- *I think you did well. There is no doubt other opportunities will present themselves to you. You are surely a hardworking girl. I have no doubt that your future is bright. Keep working hard.*

*Rerwa may have given up the pursuit of that job but not all ladies heeded that call of integrity and self-respect. It was not easy for her to get the rest of the salary. As she would call Mugabo requesting for her money, the latter would tell her that because she refused the job she is arrogant and not wise. One wonders what kind of wisdom this man is talking about. There are a number* of married men who behave like Mugabo. Is it because they are not satisfied in their homes by their wives? Even if they were not does that justify their wrongdoings? How can the government deal with such people who corrupt the dignity of women, who take away their freedom and integrity and exploit them? How can one stop this syndrome of taking advantage of poor ladies? How can one teach these men to be faithful to their wives and stop running after little girls and exploiting them and sometimes infecting them with HIV and AIDS? Eventually Mugabo gave the rest of the salary to Rerwa. By finally giving her the remainder of the money that belonged to her, Mugabo thought he was doing a favour to Rerwa whereas the latter had worked hard to earn that money. Feeling embarrassed and not wanting to meet her face to face, Mugabo transferred the money through Mobile Money. This arranged Rerwa as well. I hope the government will work hard to save many of our sisters who suffer unemployment and decide to give in to people like Mugabo. This is gender-based violence and it should never be tolerated.

By giving my monthly salary to Rerwa, I exactly wanted to fight against this situation of exploitation and abuse from some indecent men. I wanted her to be independent and responsible. Now that the project seemed to fail, I concluded that education was a weapon to fight this kind of exploitation in our country and to free Rerwa more from the likes of Mugabo. But how was she going to study without having gotten a scholarship? There was no way she would repeat her exams like Mbanda did in order to get a scholarship after the government tightened the conditions of obtaining scholarships.

There was no way, I would give up all my salary for her education and put a heavy burden to my husband when I know that the family is not just to be run by the husband but that the wife can and should assist the husband in running the family. I knew my salary was not a lot and every month we had to pay *a bank loan we obtained some years back to build our house. I always shared my experience via Skype with Mzee who was doing his studies in Rome. I knew that, having taken a vow of poverty in his religious congregation, Mzee could not do anything about Rerwa's education apart from praying for her.*

*Despite his vow of poverty that he took in the O Dei congregation, Mzee never abandoned us although we knew we should not count on him very much. He regularly kept in touch to find out how we were doing. It always pained him that he could not fulfil his role of eldest son in our family. I wonder whether he knew it before he joined because it seems to burden him despite the fact that he looks happy for the choice he has made. I was pleased to learn that his thoughts were like mine. Probably minds of the same father think alike. This is message he sent me on Skype:*

"I love Rerwa very much and I would want her to go to the university. When I realised that there was no money for school fees for Rerwa and that almost all our farms were sold and that no one knew or had revealed to us where the resulting money went, I despaired. To tell you the truth, dear sister, I did not see a solution to the problem of exploitation and lack of freedom that my other sisters might suffer were they not to go to school. The future was not going to be brighter for Rerwa who had just finished high school. Therefore, I had to attempt ways of liberating her. I was determined that she has to go to the university like the rest of us did. I commend the efforts that you have been doing already. The New Year resolution that I took was to fight so that Rerwa goes to the university. Even though I did not have her school fees, at least I had registration fees (60 US dollars). At least that would give her hope that we think about her and intend to do something for her. Without even informing you, Nadina, I told Rerwa to go and get registered to one university of her choice in the city in the hope that she was going to start the same year and if not the following year. That sounds crazy but I do not know where the belief, hope and determination came from that she will attend the university in the near future. We cannot always rely on the governments' scholarships, we have to find ways and in so doing support the government that supported us. The government has already been generous to our family. Three scholarships in the same family is a great contribution. Even if I turned my scholarship down to join religious congregation I feel indebted that I was selected and if I could I would contribute a little for my fellow countrymen to afford school.

Rerwa told me that she chose Kayiga College of Education since she wanted to become a teacher and felt it would be easy to get the job as a teacher when she graduates from the university. Even if I get school fees it would not be enough because there are other needs because of registration, school materials, bus fare etc. But I thought you would chip in despite your family commitments. I wondered how she would be walking everyday to school for four years. Since she will be at home alone –other siblings being at school – she will either have to prepare food and take it to school or not have lunch since Mbanda was still at the university and Hoza was still in high school. The former entails to cook food in the morning and to keep it warm until lunch. The walking, the cooking will make her tired even before she gets to school. This also means that she will be dozing in class because of tiredness and as a consequence her performance will be below the standard. But I did not see any other alternative. I would even thank God if I managed to get just tuition fees.

I told her that even if I manage to find school fees there is no guarantee that I will find transport money let alone money for her meals. Transport money in the city for a month is a lot especially when you have to take two buses or more or use motorbikes. Rerwa was scared and almost gave up to my offer of going to the university. What was a nice surprise almost turned out to be a cross that she was not ready to carry. I could feel for her but I saw no alternative. Thank God, there is always a way out of darkness and despair. There was a way out of what seemed a dead end. Rerwa shared with an old closest friend at high school her joy of being proposed to go to the university by her brother and also the pains it was going to entail and sought advise on whether it was worth a try.

Rerwa still remembered the whole salary you gave her for a business project that was never to succeed and she thought this intellectual project may also fail before she graduates and in the process lose another bunch of our money. Rerwa's experience of friendship teaches me that having a good friend is good but sharing your joy and sorrows to her is even better. This friend of hers –who has been studying at the same College of Education –told her not to despair and she promised to pray for her. Rerwa felt encouraged and she was ready to give it a try.

Rerwa never imagined that her friend would relate the struggle she envisioned to her parents to see if they are willing to accommodate Rerwa whom they knew since she regularly visited the family. This family was nearer to Rerwa's college compared to our home in Ndegeya. This family accepted to accommodate her for all the four years she will spend at school (if she gets the school fees, I said to myself). I could not believe it when, a few days after I requested her to register, she called me telling me that she had found a home, a family to stay in and that she would walk to school since it is not very far. This really made me realise that there are still good and caring people out there. This was already a signal that school fees will be obtained sooner or later."

*I was impressed by this story from Mzee. We did not know it but Mzee was working behind the scenes for our own good perhaps at times without success for their life style is very difficult. The family that accepted to accommodate Rerwa is just an exception to what my grandmother told me a couple of weeks ago. In a society where no one seems to care and to assist their neighbours this family is ready to take her in and bear in the cost. It is like they are willing to consider her as their own child. What a contribution it would be to Rerwa, to our family and to the nation. I wish there were families like this that are willing to assist orphans carry their heavy burden. Walking that short distance every day from this family to school is not easy either, but her perseverance through daily struggles makes Rerwa our heroine, inspiration and example. She never dreamt to go to the university as she once revealed to me but there she is now a university student. It was like a dream when Mzee made her know that he has decided that she goes to college. Having embraced the chance that she never imagined to come her way, she studies with resilience and courage. The poverty of not having all school material that are necessarily conducive for the studying environment affects her but she tries to manage with the little she has for she knows that it is a major step in her life to be where she is. We are all looking forward to a day when she will graduate and triumph over challenges.*

*Her announcement that she was accepted to stay in a nearby family was greeted by the good news that Mzee had for her. Mzee had found someone who had promised him the possibility of paying Rerwa's school fees for the first year. The promise alone was enough for an encouragement. She now knew that God was at work and He wanted her to go to the university. What started as a joke and speculation from our brother, Mzee, was becoming a reality. Rerwa's dream was coming true. Getting school fees for the first year could entail that school fees for other three years may also come.*

*The following week, the Skype conversation with Mzee went as follows:*

"While in my morning meditation, I got an idea to go to Francis, an O Dei priest and a great friend of mine –to request some money that would start a project that would make profit and eventually pay Rerwa's school fees. I was ready to sacrifice my needs for my last two months in Rome, not using my (or rather O Dei's) credit card at all – apart from toping up my oyster card so that I can take the bus or the metro to go to college in Giovani Piazza. After revealing that to Father Francis, the latter made it clear that the money of the congregation is not meant to help family members. I knew it but there was no other family to go to, there was no other friend to share my problems with. O Dei was my family and Francis and I had become friends that I considered him a member of my family. I was convinced Francis would listen and probably act. He is a good man –so many people would say of him.

Despite telling me that the congregation's money is not meant to help family members he asked me to put my request in writing and send it to him by email – so that he could keep a record, I supposed. It was this hope that I sustained and told my sister never knowing truly that it was going to materialise. I will send you the email I wrote and sent on the 31st July of that year; it was on the Feast of St Ignatius of Loyola. Giving that email on St Ignatius Feast was not just a coincidence. I was hoping that St Ignatius would intercede for me."

*Since Mzee was in high school he liked St Ignatius of Loyola and I wonder why he did not join the Jesuits, whom St Ignatius founded in the 16th century. His former schoolmates told me how he formed a group of prayers in the run up to the national exams, a group which many students –mainly finalists – attended. At the end of the prayer, Mzee would always pray to St Ignatius to intercede for those who were about to write their exams, which he was convinced St Ignatius did since all those who attended the prayers passed very well –of course after working hard.*

*Mzee would later send me the copy of the email he sent to Francis. It was entitled: A proposal. It read:*

"Dear Father,

My siblings and I have agreed to get a loan from one of the local banks in my country of 1,000 US dollars to which the family will add 500 US dollars. In fact, the meeting with the treasurer's bank is scheduled in two weeks' time. This money will help us start a business project in order to pay for Rerwa's tuition fees. Rerwa, the third child of our family, finished high school in October last year. After the sudden death of my father in March of the same year, the O Dei superiors back home generously paid school fees for Rerwa in the final year of her secondary school and they are still paying for the last born who will finish her secondary school next year.[1]

Definitely, I am aware that it is not the obligation of the congregation to pay for my sisters after our father was killed in a war that tore apart my beloved nation, but I guess, a gesture of solidarity to my family in those difficult moments. I reckon it will be impossible and beyond the capacity of the O Dei to pay for my sisters' tertiary education. Their education preoccupied me and I found it necessary to inform you. I will remain forever grateful if you can afford any help towards the business project or towards tuition fees.

Dear Father, as we wait for the business project to materialise, could you kindly assist my sister to start at least her first year of the university. By the time she finishes first year, the business project will hopefully have made some interest

---

[1]     This little sister also finished high school and she is now at the university.

that will help her attend second year. Gradually she will be able to finish her university education.

Dear Father, thank you for your cooperation. I take this opportunity to wish you a happy Feast of St Ignatius."

*Mzee would later confide in me that he never received any written response to that email from Francis. But some weeks later he was told by Francis that the latter decided to give Mzee some Euros at the end of his séjour in Rome to use to pay for his sister's tuition fees and if possible to contribute towards materialization of the project. The other good news was that Francis told Mzee that the gift of these Euros should not affect the way he used his credit card at all. He should continue to buy books and other school material. I suspect Francis did not want Mzee to find any excuse for performing poorly. Of course this meant for us his siblings that Mzee had no excuse in not bringing us gifts from Europe when he finished his program. We always looked forward to his coming home after two years of absence. Not only did we miss him for all that period but he always brought wonderful gifts to us.*

*Francis instructed his assistant to transfer the money to the O Dei's bank account in Rome from where it will be sent to the O Dei's account in Kayiga and Mzee would receive it once he reaches Kayiga. 500 € was the amount that he received from the O Dei treasurer in Kayiga. This was wonderful news for us in general and for Rerwa in particular. It is as if Francis had inquired from people in Kayiga for this amount is almost exactly the tuition fees for one academic year.*

*From the moment I heard the plans of my brother in Rome I started saving a certain percentage of my salary to chip in to that project that Mzee was thinking about. I love my husband; he is always supportive each time I bother him with family issues. When Mzee was back from Rome, I asked him to pay the 500 € he received from Francis immediately in the accounts of Kayiga*

College of Education so that Rerwa would start school the following month. I could not believe that we had already obtained school fees for the whole year even before Rerwa started the university. It was like a miracle to me that my sister was going to the university. I had never imagined it so soon.

Mzee did well to ask that the money be used to pay for the first year of Rerwa's education. It would have been difficult to invest the money had it been meant for the project. The project was going to take time to be launched since we were not able to get the loan from the local bank. This was due to Mzee's absence simply because some of the important family properties were written in his name, being the eldest in the family. We had not been able to change since he entered his congregation. Although being second oldest member of the family, family property could not be registered in my name simply because a girl marries into another family and to a certain extent loses some rights in her initial family. Therefore, some other projects are written in the name of Mbanda, the 3rd born and once Mzee comes home we will have to transfer all the official documents to Mbanda's name. Consequently, the project would have to wait but I thought Rerwa should not wait until another year to go to school. That would be to expose her to unemployment and all the consequences that come with idleness.

When Mzee came back home, he collected the land forms from the City Council. These forms proved that Mzee has replaced our father in owning the family property. Now we were ready to get the loan from the bank and to get going the business project. But since Mzee was informed by the rest of us that some farms were sold we hesitated to give the house as mortgage. Taking a loan from a bank is like a gamble. One may succeed or fail. If the gamble fails we may lose the house to the bank and that is the last thing one would want to lose in this Kayiga city no matter how simple the house would be. But life is exactly about taking chances. Qui ne risque rien ne gagne rien, the French say. Whoever does not risk *anything gets nothing. If we want to have school fees for Rerwa, one family member suggested, we had to risk and maybe risk it all. But risking the house was too much. We refused to go to the extreme of risking it all. We did not want that even the little we had be taken away. We had farms in Narame and we intended to give those as mortgage. However, the country's land registration took longer since these farms are in the village. We would have to wait maybe even more than a year.*

*Besides the credit card that Mzee had in Rome, he also received 150 Euros cash as pocket money per month. When he was thinking about the prospects of Rerwa he started saving a bit for the project so that we should not only bank on loans. Besides saving the percentage of his pocket money, Mzee saved from the journey he did to other European countries. For the 5 days he spent in Brussels and 3 days he spent in Paris and 2 days in Berlin his fellow O Dei never charged him. From the journeys he saved 250 Euros which added to other 500 Euros he had saved for two years from his pocket money. The project was almost ready to kick start since I had been saving also from my salary. A friend of Mzee, Nganga, an O Dei priest, would call this project, "Rerwa Project" and he would also give 150 Euros as his contribution to support the project. The project started very well and in fact without needing the loan from the bank.*

*The loan business lagged a lot and again it is a sign that only rich people stand better chances to get loans while they are not really the people who need the money badly like the poor do. Of course the banks want to be assured that it will get its money back. Some days ago Mzee had an interesting conversation with the bank treasurer.*

- *How many people are charged every day in courts for having failed to pay back the bank's loan? How many houses are auctioned every week because people could not*

own agreements with the bank? The bank treasurer asked
a complaining Mzee.
- Is there no way the government could bail out the poor
who have no mortgage? Mzee asked the bank treasurer.
- Go and ask the government officials, this is just the bank.
The embarrassed treasurer replied.

Mzee did not know whether he should reply the treasurer. But
normally when he feels that one talks nonsense he decides to ignore
what others say. This only confirmed that it is mostly about the
bank's interest and not the poor that banks exist. What banks and
governments ignore is that having a mortgage means that you are
not really poor. So how will a poor person then get a loan from the
bank if he wants to make any progress and bid farewell to poverty?
No one seems to care about that. No wonder those who have are
getting more and those who are poor are languishing in poverty.
But I will never give up my dream of fighting poverty most often
caused by capitalism and its selfish attitude.

We wondered which project we should undertake. From all
the money Mzee and I got from savings plus that of our friend
Nganga, we bought a motorbike to make some money in order
to get more school fees for Rerwa. This was in line with the
motorbike that we bought through the inspiration of Mbanda
some month ago. However, after one year that the motorbike had
been functioning, I came to realise that it is not easy doing such
kind of business in our country. Rich people want to get richer
quickly for it seems there is no amount of money that can satisfy a
human being. The more money the rich has the more needs and
desires he gets and consequently the more money he needs and
desires. Most of these rich people in our country are competing with
the poor. One individual could buy 20 motorbikes and give them
to people to work for him. This means motorbike conductors do
not get enough money because they claim that there are too many

bikes on the road than people need. Whereas the rich man gets a reasonable profit the poor gets almost nothing.

Our bikes are even of less capacity and efficiency compared to the big motorbike owned by the rich. Moreover, we have to pay higher taxes and we end up working for the government. As if that was not enough motorbike conductors also keep cheating the owners that it has rained the whole day and consequently they did not work. At night while they go to sleep they give the bike to others so that they get more money for themselves. While one thinks that the motorbike is being rested it is being overused. Consequently, the motorbike which you thought would function for two years only lasts for one year because of being overused and it consumes the little money you had through many repairs. We realised that our conductor was not a good person for he sold some of the bike's new parts and replaced them with old ones. We kept paying money to replace old parts. While the poor becomes poorer the rich becomes richer. The gap between the rich and the poor keeps widening.

Because of these problems that the project started encountering I started despairing. We had to give up this project half-way. We could not afford to keep losing the money. We decided to sell the motorbike just one year after it was bought. We sold it together with the motorbike that we purchased and was being run by Mbanda. That was a very painful experience that I will never forget. Thank God we had not obtained the loan from the bank otherwise we would be working for the bank's interests and reap nothing and probably not enough for the bank's interests. Besides the problematic motorbikes, we had other sources of income. Dear father, the farms you sold had not been taken completely by owners and thus Don, our stepmother, kept farming and harvesting. But this was never going to last because the owners wanted to own their farms completely. Owners were happy to see their land in fallow and did not want us to think we still owned the land or had some shares on it. It is now five years since they asked Don to stop cultivating there. Yet they haven't built anything on that land. They are not grateful to you for having sold the farms to them let alone compassionate to your children.

Moreover, the cow that you left has grown fast. It has given birth twice and we hope to sell one to pay the rest of Rerwa's fees. This famous cow is a sign of love from you dad. I heard that one of your brothers refused to lend you money for medication but he was ready to buy the cow when you offered it out for sale. When you realised that your own brother loved money more than he loved you, you changed your mind and gave up on selling the cow. You revealed that you would prefer to die and leave the cow for your own children rather than give it to him. All the above shows that humankind is a selfish animal that always wants to progress at the expense of others or that wants to be ahead of others even if they are his relative. Francis and Nganga are just an exception to the rule. It is a pity that some of our relatives kept troubling us that the cow was supposed to give them milk and that we should know that we have to share it. I wonder what kind of logic they use to reason. That is a sign of obsession about properties.

There is no doubt that despite these challenges, Rerwa will one day graduate from College of education. In the meantime, there is wonderful news that Rerwa will get married soon to her fiancé. They have now started all preparations for the three types of wedding that we have: civil wedding by the mayor, traditional wedding and religious wedding by a priest. All of us are really excited for this occasion and are happy for Rerwa. We are going to support Rerwa and her fiancé as much as we can. In our culture, a girl plans all the traditional wedding since it takes place at the girl's family. People accompanying the bridegroom come to the house of the bride to give dowry to the family of the bride. It is indeed an interesting ceremony. Although it is a good occasion, it consumes a lot of money for both the bridegroom and the groom.

*Besides the little money Rerwa earned here and there as I told you in the previous emails, she never had any other chance of working. This means that it is all up to me to find some millions to organise the whole ceremony. I feel happy for Rerwa but at the same time I feel stressed and not sure what to do. But I have a feeling that things will turn out well. How we wish you and mum could attend physically that wedding. Kindly pass this wonderful news to our mother.*

*With lots of Love,*
*Nadina.*

# Thank you

Nadina's father cannot believe that so many good things have happened to his children. It seems like the Leader where Hachris lives does some magic to help those that are left behind. Hachris can only thank those who have worked selflessly to make his children be where they are. Love is a key in taking care of fellow human beings. In his next email, he urges people to revive this love.

*Our Leader is really a loving and a good force as we call him here. I do not know how to describe him or her (he is neither a man nor a woman). But being a man and having been influenced by the male hegemony when I was on the other side and not wanting to confuse you with the he or she, allow me dear Nadina, to use he. Our Leader does not necessarily tell us what He does to loved ones who are still at your side but I am sure that He is the one who is behind the good that you guys have been experiencing and doing. He does not force anyone to behave the way they do. But like a sunshine attracts those who sees it He attracts people of good will towards Him freely. I thank all those people who have a generous heart and help out orphans to achieve what their heart desires. I am happy that Rerwa has gone to the university also. She did not seem as sharp as the other kids but I am sure she will make it in due time. I cannot find words to express my happiness when I heard about her wedding. I wish her all the best. Hopefully, she will also be blessed with a wonderful husband who loves her, cares for her and assists her in all family endeavours. I wish them all the best things that a parent could wish their kids. I wish them prosperity and to live together forever. I wish them to have lovely kids. I have no doubt that Rerwa is going to make an amazing wife, a wonderful mother to her kids, a caring wife to her husband. It is a pity that I am not around to organise that wedding and you have to struggle with the little money you have. I really wonder how you manage all these things when you already have two kids to take care of without counting your needs and those of your husband.*

*Dear Nadina, you are really incredible. Saving some money from your salary not just for your children but for your siblings is really a sign of love you have for your siblings. I wish some of my own brothers and sisters had the same love when we were there. You heard it from people how one of my brothers even preferred my cow to my health as you mentioned to me in the last email. We did not really show that love to each other as we were supposed to. My mother used to say that some of her sons are selfish. Please keep that love and it will be your shield against all evils in that other side of the river and it will make all the difference. Shortly before I left your place for this beautiful land, I realised that love became too secularised and consequently lost its power and meaning. I wish through the power of journalism and the example you give to your siblings you could revive that spirit of love. I am happy you are already doing that, acting like a fire that is kindling other dwindling fires.*

*I cannot really find words to thank you for what you have done for you siblings. I was not wrong to place my hope and trust in you. I am glad that you did it even far better than I anticipated. You have been a person who knows how to sacrifice the little you have so that you can put a smile on the face of other kids. When it came to your siblings you gave almost everything you had. You gave up the pleasure you and your family would have enjoyed and you assisted them. Thank you for being you where we needed you the most. Thank you for representing me. There is no doubt that in the near future, all your siblings will start their only families and will no longer burden you. As we wait for that moment, we thank you for having left an unforgettable mark to our family, your family. May you be rewarded hundred times.*

*I thank Mzee as well for taking various initiative and working hard for the promotion and prosperity of our family. In a special way, I thank the O Dei very much. I hope my son will grow to be a generous priest like Francis and many others. Having worked for them, I realised that priests really make a big difference to the world. I am sure our Leader is proud of them. Of course it is not all of them who are sincere in their ministry. Some have disgraced their career and have caused scandals of all kinds. But we should learn to focus on the good that has taken place rather than wanting to shadow it with the evils of the minority.*

*P.S: Please next time tell me how Rerwa and Hoza finished high school because I left when they were still studying in high school. Relate to me how Kayiga looks like as well and whether my children still live there.*

98

# Tweeter message

—•—

Behind the scenes Mzee worked hard to ensure his sisters finished at least high school. When they finished high school it was a big celebration for all of us because so many are those who drop out of school when their parents pass away simply because there is no one willing or ready to take care of their school fees. The family congratulated Rerwa and Hoza for being courageous women and asked them never to give up their dreams but that the sky was the limit. Mzee celebrate in style since he is the engineer behind their high school achievement. This is the Twitter and Facebook status I saw on Mzee's account relating how he had managed to get school fees for our sisters:

*When my father died, I decided to speak to the superior of the O Dei in my country, Father Auka, that there was no way that Rerwa and Hoza could finish high school knowing that Nadina was still at the university and Mbanda was a simple cook. Without hesitation Father Auka agreed that he will source some money for them since they were not far from finishing. Rerwa was already in her final form (senior 6) while Hoza was in senior 4 of high school. Father Auka sourced the money —I do not know from where —and my sisters finished high school. Each semester they would go to see the bursar of the O Dei to get school fees. Hoza was even lucky to get global fund –courtesy of Don – to pay her for the upkeep at school. Hoza generously shared that money for upkeep with her sister for few needs. After both finished, they would go together to thank Father Auka for his generosity in particular and the O Dei in general.*

This gesture from Mzee lifted some burden from Nadina's shoulders. She only had to find food for her siblings to eat before and after school and some transport money.

"May God bless those who generously spared what they had for those beautiful ladies to finish high school" were some words of those who commented or retweeted on Mzee's status.

- There is no doubt that these O Dei priests are some of the people who are making my dream of fighting poverty come true, Nadina wrote in her diary.

# Kayiga: A city for the rich?

~━•━⌒

This morning Nadina has decided to reply to another of her father's question: The progress of Kayiga, the capital of their country.

*Dearest Father,*

*I wonder whether you would now recognize Kayiga if you re-cross the river. Even if you recognize it you would admire the changes that have taken place in such short time just like many foreigners get surprised when they come to visit. You would compare it with the time when at a young age you came to Kayiga when the big part was a bush and an animal jungle and would realise that there is no similarity left. From ashes of wars and conflict, a good city is being built. My husband and I live in the Western part of the country where both of us work. Even me I must confess that each time I go to Kayiga I realise that it changes every time for the better.*

*So many roads are being built and expanded. To reduce traffic a number of roads have been connected with new ones and thus short cuts have been created. Other roads have been turned into one-way. Since it is just the beginning people are still getting lost. Kayiga is trying to imitate cities of developed nations by increasing skyscrapers. Investors have been given a leeway to* invest in construction. Companies have benefited by renting these new building and making modern day offices. Roundabouts are created, names of all roads added, quarters for rich people built and names of localities changed to suit modern day thinking and to break away with the past that divided our people. It is very exciting indeed to see how much and fast Kayiga is changing. If God grants us peace and good leaders who do not just care about their selfish interests in twenty years our capital city will be one of the best on the continent.

Some people believe that as Kayiga changes for the better at the same time it also changes for worse. Is this a contradiction or an oxymoron? There are many changes that take place there including major changes. Although complex houses are built day and night and Kayiga is becoming a city in construction; a kind of construction site, poor people are not fairly treated. Most of them leave the city without much compensation. Most importantly, Kayiga is becoming more expensive and indeed the second most expensive city in the region. Our leaders want Kayiga to become a regional hub but they should also think of ways to accommodate all classes in the city. Economic development is excellent but it become very problematic when it excludes a certain group of people.

Dear father, as a wise man, you saw this radical change coming long time ago. Consequently, you started concentrating on Narame –in the countryside – rather than Ndegeya in Kayiga. I hear that is why you sold some farms in Kayiga and used part of the money to buy farms and to build a house in Narame. Despite the progress in Kayiga, many people wonder whether some of the progress is not exaggerated as if we have gone to live to another planet or have become extraterrestrial or lost touch with reality because the rich have simply completely ignored the poor.

When I went to London for a journalism conference, I was amazed at the fact that even people in suits at times prefer to *cycle to get to various destinations. It is even healthier they would say than to always seat in a bus or in a personal vehicle or in an underground tube. But in Kayiga, at least in most parts,* chez les nouveaux riches *–newly rich people, no one can use their bicycles lest his bicycle is confiscated by the police. It is simply not allowed and in fact an offence to ride a bicycle in those parts unless it is a sports bike –yet this can only be owned by rich people because the poor cannot afford it.*

*In a similar vein, small shops have been destroyed. Those who resisted and sell their items in their hands should be wary of being arrested by police. They are always running away when they see the police. Some of these people lose their items with customers when policemen come close to where they sell their items. If these customers are generous enough to return the items they do not know to whom it belonged. Many poor people in Kayiga wake up only to be told that they have to relocate to the countryside to give way to big companies and Multinational Corporations that have purchased their land –the government's land as a matter of fact. Capitalism and free market are taking over the country but they are making lots of casualties on their way. Maybe this is how many big cities have developed and this is the cost the poor person has to pay. In his wisdom, one singer sang it very well in the 50s that* "Kayiga, happy are those who will see you in the years to come, but alas and poor are those who will run towards you in the future". *This future has become the present. No more farming in the city. Therefore, many people who used to make a living on agriculture had to leave Kayiga to its suburbs or to neighbouring provinces for them to survive. But who should one blame or condemn? Those who develop the city? The poor themselves who cannot compete? Does development not necessarily have to come with some of these costs? Is it not possible to develop and at the same time carry the poor along?*

*Stubbornly, my siblings are still in Kayiga and do not expect to move anytime soon unless it either becomes too precarious or* they are moved by force. Then I will be obliged to take them to the Eastern part of the country or bring them to my house. But I hope the latter situation will not happen since I do not want to make it obvious to everyone that I have become the father to my siblings. I normally want to do it quietly and from afar. I am sure many people wonder how they survive and how they managed to go to the university. Since I rarely visit them –because nowadays they spend most of their time at the university –, I make sure I put little money I save on their bank account. It is them who visit me when they are on holiday. This new development serves me better as well. With my work, studies and kids at home I cannot afford to be going to Ndegeya many times. I have managed to keep my promise of phoning them every day. They are managing generally well despite the tough life in Kayiga.

They no longer use firewood to cook like when you were still there. Like many people in Kayiga, they have now resorted to charcoal and probably when Electricity Company produces enough electricity for people in the city, they may have to think of using electric stoves to safeguard the environment from which all of us benefit. Gas will be another option since it is extracted in the country's biggest lakes. But this depends on whether foreigners will not exploit it all for themselves as they sometimes do and accumulate all the resources they get from some of our poor nations with the complicity of few elites who betray their fellow countrymen.

To push further my earlier questions: Who can be sad that development is coming in Kayiga? Who still complains that they were chased from the city? Is this not how other big cities like New York and Rome developed? If we are to embrace the values that 2050 vision brings should we not be ready for sacrifices and the cost that economic development brings about? But should development be at the expense of the poor? Is there no way of including the poor in making decisions that will affect their life *and progress together with everyone? Why does the government not establish forums for people to dialogue and see the consequences and effects of certain decisions? How can the government provide safety nets for the poor? How can the elites take interest in other people's interests?*

*Manzi is a friend of mine who works for the city council. I always ask him above and similar questions whenever he comes to visit our family but he has never given me convincing answers. Sometimes I tend to agree with Gasa, our former neighbour who, once annoyed with politicians and their sometimes silly decisions, would proclaim:* "La Politique c'est l'art de mentir" *– Politics is the art of cheating. Gasa is convinced that most politicians make rhetorical promises when they are campaigning but they hardly fulfil ¾ of what they promise. Once they get the comfort that power brings them they tend to forget what they promised. They are more interested in what they gain and less in the interest of those they represent. They do not take interest in the interests of those they govern. More often than not, they simply betray the trust of the electorate. I recall an interesting discussion I once had with Gasa.*

- *How many members of parliament come back to their constituencies to consult local people on issues that affect their lives before they make laws that affect the very people who have elected them? Gasa asked me.*
- *I have never seen a single member of parliament in my constituency. I had never thought about that. What I realise is that when it is time for re-election these members of parliament come back smiling to the people who trusted them before so as to apply their art of cheating once again. I added after reflecting.*
- *You see that now you are even quoting me. Gasa said jokingly. You are repeating to a certain extent what I told*

*you months ago. Rhetorically, these outgoing members of parliament will say that change is not something that one can achieve in a fortnight. As a result, they tell people that they need a second chance to continue the changes they have started. They convince people on how not voting for them will be to become an enemy of change and to betray the little progress they have already helped the people to achieve.*

- *That is right. They go on to show a past that was worse than the present and cheat illiterate citizens who have fear of the future and do not want to go back to that terrible past. Citizens do not even see that the present was supposed to be far better than it is. It is only lack of initiatives from some of the leaders, selfish interests, corruption, nepotism that caused this present to almost resemble the terrible past. Unfortunately, my fellow journalists purposely ignore this reality since some of them are instruments of some leaders and benefit from their corrupt behaviours.*

- *When the vote is cast in favour of these members of parliament –although grudgingly- and the second term that was given to the leader comes to an end, citizens feel betrayed twice but it is too late to change anything. The leader is happy to have made enough profit to take care of himself and his family for the rest of his life. He knew that the constitution does not allow him another term and therefore it does not matter if he messes up for he is not going to ask anyone to vote for him again. Gasa concluded.*

*I could really see that Gasa was not happy and rightly so. When I tell this to Manzi –a member of parliament for a locality in the Western part of the country –, he does not believe me, I guess because he realises that I have found out what he and his colleagues do. Fortunately, we are very good friends and we cannot stop being friends just because I have committed a crime of calling reality in its real name. But there is need for change, not the kind of change that the politicians mentioned above talks about during the time of campaign but change that will transform even the politician understanding of change. Not simply the change of infrastructure, the change of hearts of politicians and decision makers so that they can take into consideration the poor. To achieve that we all have to examine our conscience. If that happens, Kayiga will accommodate people of all backgrounds instead of being hostile to them. One of the country's Prime Minister rightly said that we cannot afford to build a city for only the rich. Hopefully, leaders will heed the call of the Prime Minister and the current Prime Minister together with his team will do all that is in their powers to fight for justice and equality.*

*Dear father, next time I will take some pictures of mostly transformed areas of Kayiga and send them to you. I have no doubt that you will be shocked by the transformation that has taken place.*

*That is it for today, if you have some questions do not hesitate to ask me in your next email.*

# A Stepmother aunt

The emails that Nadina sends to her father have become an opportunity to evaluate the kind of life that they lived and to remember some of the steps of her life. One of the issues that she does not normally talk about much with other people is that she had a stepmother who lived with them for a while. For the last couple of days, she has been reading her diary. She was struck to realise how much impact having a step mother has had on her life and the life of her siblings. Today, she decides to relive some of the moments and at the same time share them with his father in an email.

*Dear father, although I was too young to know the importance of it, I felt for you when our mother died and you stayed without a partner at such an early age when you were beginning to appreciate the sweetness of married life. You became patient enough so as to let us grow first before you could even think of bringing someone else in our lives who may open the scars of a yet to heal wound of losing our loved mother at such a tender age and in unknown and painful circumstances of war. I admired your wisdom as you willingly embraced the suffering that comes with losing a partner at such an early age of marriage. Your rationality and love triumphed on passions and desires.*

*The death of our mother is a symbol of all those many people who perished in wars and conflicts here in our country and those who are still losing their innocent lives on our continent. We remember especially those innocent lives that lost their lives in the genocide against Tutsi in our neighbouring country Rwanda. I wish everyone with a human heart could fight hard to stop the death of innocent people. I wish politicians of all calibres, from our nation and outside, from our continent and outside, could cooperate with a united heart and mind to bring about justice and peace to our beloved continent. I dream of a time when no child will be made an orphan, when no parent will be made single by the brutality of other human beings, when no parent will be left as if he never gave birth. I dream of a time when all children will be allowed to go to school in peace and to have enough food, a time when our parents will work in an environment where they do not hear the noise of the gun and are assured that their children will grow to reach eighty.*

*Ten years after our mother's death, you thought we had grown up a bit to stand in our home the presence of a woman who is not our mother. You married Don as your second wife. She was supposed to live with us and to probably continue what mother had started and where she left. Unlike my siblings, I always played indifferent and clever on that second marriage. I remember when just after our house was handed back to us again by those who had occupied it after the civil war you asked me together with Mzee to go and prepare the room for she was coming home that night to be your wife. Just like that.*

*Don was the elder sister of our late mother. She never got married but she had one child. She had been living with our grandmother not far from our house. By marrying her, it meant our aunt became our stepmother and we her nephews and nieces became her stepchildren. When we would visit our grandmother, my siblings used to say and sing that they can never tolerate a stepmother for she would not be their mother. Don listened to some of those songs and would react negatively as if she knew that she was going to become our stepmother at some point. I always asked myself these questions: was she really our stepmother? Could we just have regarded her as our aunt and nothing more nothing less? Should parents wait until their children have become independent for them to bring in other wives for the sake of the children's psychological development? To the first question I thought Don was just like our mother, with the same blood like us. To the last question, I answered yes for children need to be brought up in a conducive environment lest they adopt bad behaviours later in life. But is it just about the children's right? Is their right absolute? What happens if it conflicts with the father's right to have another partner? Surely any one has a right to remarry when their partner dies. But most often it is the male that seems to ensure he gets remarried. Female manage to stay on their own up to old age and death. When parents' right conflict with children's right, there is no doubt that one right will override the other but I wonder whose? Who decides which right to override which one?*

*Father, in your wisdom, you spared us that curse and trouble of a stepmother for you married, Don, our mother's elder sister. I always called her my aunt and never my stepmother. Maybe I never appreciated the notion of a stepmother and was trying to put myself in safe waters. Don worked hard for us for the ten years we lived together despite shortcomings that are part of any human nature.*

*You remember she has her child also and that meant this child would automatically become part of us. I still wonder how you considered her. As your child? Your stepchild? What did that mean and entail for you and for her? In my eyes, she remains my cousin sister. She never acquired a new status from the fact that her mother was married to you. May be that was a mistake on my part. Two families in one house were suddenly supposed to become one. I knew that coexistence between these two families was never going to be easy. I always told you that we run a risk of turning relatives into enemies. I am not in a position to answer those questions because I was never home apart from holiday times in all those ten years since I attended a boarding school. My siblings who lived with the other family on a daily basis know better and they will tell you their own stories when they get the chance of using the Internet. Each time I came back home I would realise that two camps had created themselves, the one of my siblings and the one of Don and her child. The two families never became one, they remained two. Maybe that was a genuine way of confronting reality.*

*Despite shortcomings that characterised the coexistence, myself I thank Don a lot for everything she did for me, for my siblings and for you father. I remember when I went to senior 4, after passing my O' Levels with a distinction and coming first in the entire school, I was sent to another school far from the first and from our house. You were unemployed at that time and I wondered whether I would not be compelled to drop out of school due to lack of school fees. So I would call Don to communicate my needs to you but I knew she would provide all that I needed, which most of the times she did. I thought I would pay back once I finish and get a good job. She even used to visit me every year bringing me loaves of bread, fruits and some money. On some occasions, she even paid school fees for me. That meant a lot to me. It was my life that was being rescued; the foundation of my life was being laid down. I wonder what I can repay her for her goodness to me and I guess to my siblings.*

*When I finished high school, again with a distinction, and second in the entire school, I wrote her a letter of thanks for all she did for me. She was like a mother to me. Although she never replied that letter, I knew she was happy that my heart beat with gratitude for what she has done. In her quietness, she admired me. I admired her as well. Unlike my brother Mbanda, after my first attempt of national exams I got a scholarship to the National University where I studied journalism. Unlike my brother Mzee who declined the scholarship because his heart was on becoming a priest, I was happy to go to the university where I met the love of my life. After teaching at a high school in Kayiga for a year, I then started the university.*

*In the meantime, Mzee who had joined the O Dei in the Western part of our country was finishing his two years of novitiate. There his heart was taught to master the virtues and behaviour of the O Dei so that he does not feel a stranger to the organisation as he moves in various steps and ranks of the organisation. When Mzee completed two years in the novitiate he was admitted to take vows of poverty, chastity and obedience. You remember that yourself, Don, Mbanda and I attended his vows ceremony together with his friend Pam. After Mzee finished pronouncing his vows, I could not help but shed tears. I imagined my brother not having to get married and not having children of his own. What a handsome man wasted. How many beautiful ladies have been fighting to possess him? I wondered. Could he not still have served God in other better ways? But what God has chosen, no one else would have. I congratulated him but he knew I was not happy with his decision. But still I could not mince my words.*

- *Why did you really decide to join O Dei dear brother? Don't you realise that our family is very poor and needs your contribution? I asked him.*
- *Everyone is free to make their own decisions, he murmured. I believe the best gift God gave to us is to be free beings. He retorted.*
- *Ok. I understand. Mzee, be happy, I replied.*

*Although Don admired me, I do not think she admired the other siblings who lived with her all the times. Things seem to have deteriorated after you passed away. My siblings would tell me –I do not know to what extent this was true – how at some point, Don and her child used to cook food and eat alone and my siblings would go hungry. She always believed that I and Mzee sent them some money. Where would a university student get money from? I was struggling to get money to print my notes or buy syllabuses. Moreover, I thought she would understand the vow of poverty that Mzee took in her presence. Maybe she did not understand that since the vows were pronounced in German but I remember Father Mart translated it for our parents some of whom never knew the language of the Whiteman. But who on earth understands that vow of poverty anyway? Do all religious people who take it understand it let alone living up to its expectations? I have been wondering. You always see them driving big cars. They are always travelling from countries to countries.*

*Mzee told us that their superior in the novitiate told them that everyone should adapt his own way of living poverty as long as he remains within the norms. It is very hard for us let alone other people to understand that Mzee took a vow of poverty when we see him fly out of the country for studies to various countries of Africa and to Europe or America just for studies, studies which do not seem to end. No wonder Don thought Mzee had a lot of money. It was hard to comprehend that he had taken a vow of poverty while she sometimes saw him drive a car each time he would come home to visit us. But we ordinary people ignore that these people's poverty is apostolic in the sense that it helps them do their mission well. One goes to study so as to change the world, one drives that car not for luxury, I hope, but mainly to minister to the people of God wherever they are. At least this is what I could remember from the interviews I had with some priests and nuns.*

Besides many of them look simple people despite their high quality education. They live in simple houses.

I suppose Mzee understood poverty even more when he went to study in Zimbabwe where he was a billionaire but was not able to buy a loaf of bread with one billion of Zimbabwe dollars. The little pocket money that he was given would devalue by the end of the week sometimes by the end of the day. I remember reporting on TV that Zimbabwe had the highest inflation in the world in a long time. To cope with inflation the chief of the Zimbabwe Reserve Bank would order that they slash three zeros at the same time on a billion dollar note but in a month the change would almost seem ineffective and inefficient. I remember on his first return from Zimbabwe, Mzee brought us notes of billions to keep as our record.

With time, I realised that the coexistence between our aunt and us had become sour and almost impossible. She started turning into our stepmother for real. She became more a stepmother than an aunt. Don would at times enter into arguments with Hoza, Mzee and Mbanda who seem not to be introvert like me and Rerwa. Hoza, being a little different and sharper than all of us could not keep quiet when she feels treated unjustly and her rights trampled upon. She would respond without much hesitation. Don would always tell me, when I would be back for holidays, how Mbanda had become the cause of family tensions. This may have been true since Mbanda saw himself as the one responsible of what was taking place and the defender of his sisters' rights and freedom, and the guarantor of their peace and happiness. Maybe he was touched when he heard how they were treated and vowed to fight for their independence. With this experience, with its ups and downs, I have come to confirm that no one, no matter how related you are, can ever replace your mother. "A stepmother is never your mother", as my sisters would sing.

*Despite the good thing that Don did to us, to our father and to myself in particular, I looked forward to her going back where she belonged before she came to our house eleven years ago, after learning that my siblings had become unhappy with her and her child —and grandchild since her child had given birth in the process. Mbanda keeps reminding us that it was fortunate that she never married legally to our father. The torment would even have been greater. Legal marriage gives one the right to the part or full property of one's husband and somehow automatically to the way one treats children. If there was an injustice it would have been difficult to restore it without going to the judges, had Don been legally married to you father. Imagine children accusing their aunt in the court of law or vice versa. Although similar incidences are not uncommon, we did not wish them to happen to us. But taking it from Don's perspective it would have been fairer if she was legally married to you so that she could enjoy some benefits of marriage.*

*Maybe Don was right to take a hardliner stand since at some point she was no longer getting much money from you my father since you decided to go and stay in Narame. Having realised that life in Kayiga was very expensive, you wanted Don to come with you to Narame but she would not understand. From then onward, you rarely came back to Kayiga. Mzee told me that he would call you to inquire why you decided to distance yourself from family business in Kayiga. He had vowed to come and grill you in a heated debate, with all his Political Science after obtaining his degree and prize in Political Science. That was never going to be for destiny has its own ways. The terrible war would take you away from us and Mzee will always curse the earth for taking your life few months before he met you, saw you and discussed with you family issues.*

*Living with Don in your absence even made us realise how important your love was. The love you showed us after our beloved mother had gone before us to the land of our ancestors is an unforgettable testimony of a parent who gives everything he is and has to his children. Not only did you have to bear the burden of a loving father you added the challenges that a mother faces; cooking, doing laundry, fetching water. It was unbelievable that you could manage all those things. Since I was the only teen girl you taught me how to do household tasks, so that once in a while I would assist you and take some burden from you. At least I could iron your clothes, cook for my siblings when you would have gone to work. This love you had for us remained unchanged even in times of suffering and poverty. You quickly learnt to be our mother and remained a good loving father to us. The most important lesson of my life I learnt from you. You taught me how to become a father to my siblings. I believe you died loving us. You died happy, though in your son's absence.*

*Even though your passing away was very sudden, it seems you knew that you would not survive the injuries you sustained from the gunshots of a destructive war. You told people that you were now ready to go since I am there I could take care of my brother and sisters. When I heard this from Mrs Vest, the wife of my uncle, I laughed and wondered how I was going to do that. God has a sense of humour indeed. Thank you for being a good teacher to me. It seems I have not failed so far. I will keep trying.*

# Worst day of (my) life

━━•━━

Mzee has now spent twenty years of his life as an O Dei. He confessed that this is the kind of life he always desired. It is what his heart always longed for. It is what he chose and he is happy with his choice. As you know he promised to live his entire life in the O Dei. He discovered their talents, their success worldwide and admired the way they kept their fire burning reaching out to many people in need. O Dei priests are involved among other things in education at all levels, work for justice and faith; they work with people of all kinds throughout the world. O Dei make one of the most sophisticated and important institutions in the Catholic Church. However, the O Dei is made of ordinary people most of them from ordinary and humble backgrounds. Some of them have weaknesses like anyone of us. This is no surprise because they are just human beings like all of us.

When Nadina and her siblings celebrated the fifteenth anniversary of their father's passing on to the other side of the river, Mzee told those present his experience, an experience that Nadina has documented very well as a journalist:

*"Dear siblings,*
*Dear Distinguished guests,*

*today*

*I thank the O Dei for what they did to me and what they spent on me and my siblings. On the day my beloved father finished his journey on this earth, the rector of my college, Father Sima quickly bought me a ticket and the priest I lived with for five years in the same house, Father Lada whisked me off to the airport so that I come and give my father a befitting final respect and farewell worthy of a loving father. On that ill-fated day, just after classes, Father Sima had asked me how my father was doing and I had said that he was responding to medication after the operation and the removal of the bullet the previous day not knowing that he had just passed away to the land of the living dead. On that worst day, in the morning, during Mass, I thanked the Lord for a successful operation that took many hours the previous night. Fifty minutes after speaking to Father Sima, I learnt the news from my cousin who is a doctor that my father had just breathed his last and passed on to the other side. I had to quickly call Father Sima. I never saw him before sympathising like on that day – a day that went down in history as the worst day of my life. He never knew what to tell me and how to present his condolences. His hug was like of a father consoling his son. I was a good friend of his. He was a mentor to me, one of the best teachers I have ever met. He wishes the best in me. He always encouraged me.*

*After learning the worst news ever, I spent the rest of the afternoon in company of fellow O Dei (Kayigi and Bujado) whom my family knew very well. Kayigi brought me some airtime to call people and inform them of the sad news and Bujado handed me a note of 50 US dollars to accompany me on my journey. This was lot of money taking into consideration that we received 80 US dollars as our pocket money. At night, both accompanied me to the airport together with Father Lada to catch a flight to Kayiga.*

*Shortly after they left me, I became aware that I was on my own. My misery was only beginning. I felt like a part of me was taken away from me. I wondered where and by whom. I was so weak like never before. I actually heard a voice telling me, "Young man, you are on your own," just like the main actor in Slumdog Millionaire movie was told when he was about to answer his final question. No one was there to help him like they did in previous questions. So was I, nobody was there to help me in any way not even console me on my way back home. In the waiting room at the International Airport I called a friend of mine Consolata to inform other former schoolmates and classmates that my father had passed away. Then came the long journey from Har to Kayiga via Nambi. I had done that journey many times before but it never felt that long. It felt longer than the journey I did some months earlier from Kayiga to Rome.*

*To distract myself, I would lean to the window but I could only see darkness all over. There was no one in the plane to console me. It was all quiet. Maybe if it were not a vow of poverty I would have got someone to accompany me and to share in my misery. But flights are very expensive no one will blame the O Dei for letting me go alone. They had done their best because some congregations do not even give their members a chance to go and bury their loved ones if their relatives live very far.*

*In that moment of darkness, many thoughts came to my mind. The first and persisting thought was "young man this is the end of your religious life, your father is gone and you have to take care of your siblings, Nadina can't do it on her own. She is just a lady. And remember you are the first born. Do not run away from your responsibilities". I would not listen to that discouragement instead I would try to chat with people next to me but they seemed not interested, they felt sleepy and who knows they might have had their own problems and difficulties that could have been even bigger than mine but they would not disclose to a stranger.*

*I reached Kayiga International Airport in the morning at 8:30hrs exhausted not having slept for the past two days pondering the fate of my beloved father whose voice had suddenly changed and had become terribly weak when I spoke to him on the phone three days earlier before he passed away to the world of the living dead. All this was to prepare me to his sudden death. But still, I could not believe what had happened to my father. At some point, I thought the whole process was a dream. At other times I thought I was watching an action movie. I believed that my father was dead but I seemed not convinced. What is life that we should care for it? I wondered. How can someone who seemed okay today disappear the following day and go for good? Is he really gone? Gone, but where to? Will he ever be back? On my arrival to Kayiga, I was consoled to see a cohort of people, former classmates and schoolmates, siblings and family relatives and friends from all corners of the country who had come to present their condolences to me. After all I was not on my own. When I saw these people who had come to comfort me, I felt strong and loved in those difficult moments. I was able to appreciate the gift of friendship and the impact it can have on one's life.*

*While still at the airport, I called the superior of the O Dei in my country, Father Auka. He invited me to the provincial house to make plans for the funeral. I went there, took shower and entered his car to Narame where the funeral Mass and burial would be held. He handed me an envelope with some money for receiving those who came for the funeral as it is in our culture. In our culture we do not take long to bury the dead. We do not need to gather money first to make a big celebration. Some societies are known to keep the dead body for the whole year sourcing money to celebrate the deceased. Besides that money they spend on the celebration day, they have to keep paying the mortuary. There is no doubt that this impoverishes more those who are poor. For us a simple funeral is allowed. What matters is the love and respect that you show to the person who dies. But even if the culture of sourcing money was part of my country, it would not have been possible in that period of war. I am sure my dad would not mind that we held a simple funeral for him.*

*As some of you would remember very well, my father's funeral Mass was controversial and some people —those whom I believe want to show that they are more Catholics than the Pope —never received communion for they felt that was a Mass for a dead pagan which was not supposed to have been said in the first place. Were they jealous that the family had brought their own priest from Kayiga, that we were independent in a way from the local parish? Who are they to judge others? Were they jealous that there was going to be a priest in our family? As it is the custom of the Catholic Church when a priest from another diocese wants to say Mass in another parish that is not his own, Father Auka had called the parish priest, Father Ruber, to request permission to say that Mass. Father Auka even explained to the crowd that we received permission but people would not listen. I wonder why.*

*Surprisingly, the same Father Ruber would refuse us the permission to say Mass five months later on the occasion of laying the tomb stone saying that we were actually not supposed to say the funeral Mass in the first place. This was simply because our beloved father was considered a pagan having not had a religious wedding ceremony with Don —our aunt and former stepmother. I begged Ruber who probably was known to my father and who knew him, and explained in my little theology and commonsense that if someone has died he should not be refused Mass for Mass is exactly meant to pray for the dead and to ask mercy for God. Who are we to judge other beings? How can one know what goes in the heart of another being? Can anyone pretend to know the secret relation one has with God? What if my father had reconciled with God shortly before he died? I get surprised that some Catholics believe and argue that we should not say Mass for "pagan" people. My father wasn't a* pagan; he was just not married religiously. Even if he were a pagan that was exactly the moment to pray for him as our faith allows.

I for one I believe that these Catholics and some conservative priests who think in that way are like the Pharisees in the gospel. The same Pharisees were not happy with Jesus that he was dining and wining with those they branded sinners. Yet Jesus told the Pharisees clearly that he came for the sick and not for the healthy since it is logically the former who need a doctor and not the latter. It is surprising that those who are supposed to preach the gospel behave like the Pharisees, whose behaviour they are supposed to despise. Unfortunately, the pharisaic attitude becomes their way of life. They become sick also like those sinners but unlike sinners they deny that they are sick, and for Jesus that denial is a grave sin; it is a serious sickness that even prevents one from being healed.

I have an impression that Catholics who behave in such a pharisaic way seem to contradict their faith. How on earth can they believe in praying for all souls departed so that God will have mercy on them and at the same time they refrain from praying for them? To me, they seem worse than Protestants who have protested clearly and publicly that they cannot pray for someone who is dead. Father Auka, a theologian and once a rector of an O Dei college of theology, laughed at the decision of Father Ruber and the behaviour of these ignorant Catholics. But diplomatically he did not want to criticise them in public.

I enjoyed the funeral Mass for I took the opportunity to reconcile with my father and God himself. Initially I condemned my father for having chosen to put on such a short fight to the bullet and to go just like that without waiting for me. I was angry with God who called him so prematurely. I had decided to quit O Dei because I had just lost my faith. Although I was not present to accompany my father in his agony and when he passed way to the other side of the world, I tried to keep strong. I even tried to smile to people who had come for the funeral. Our enemies did not believe *it and were sad to see myself and my siblings smile on the day of our father's moving on. When I left the country where I was studying, I was given the task to come and console the family. That was my chief motive even before some people gave it to me as an advice.*

*When I told the doctor who announced me my father's death to wait for me before the funeral he did not believe that it would be possible for me to come all the way from Har city. When Don saw me she cried together with my other aunties who were sitting where my father's body lied. I smiled at them as if to tell them that they should not despair and that death can never have the last word on life. I consoled them but in vain. So did I console my sisters who were crying when they were laying my father to rest and put soil on the casket —a casket that I volunteered to carry to the grave as my last gesture of respect and love to my father. Despite my consoling them, I was also crying inside and made my agony heard by those close to me when my father's body was being moved down into the grave.*

*I never understood what was going on. I thought I would wake up from that dream but it seems it was reality. Will I never see my father again on this earth, receive advice from him, a hug from him? I never imagined how my celebrations and triumphs as I become a priest of God will never be his and shared with him. I could not imagine how I will never see him smile again. A friend of mine interjected when I informed him of my father's passing away.*

- *"Oh lala, your father is gone without celebrating with you the day of your priesthood".*
- *That is destiny my friend. We cannot change it. We just have to accept it. I answered.*

*As the body was being buried under the ground, after I just put a little soil on his casket, I never understood where my father went. I never understood death and how it works. Someone who has lived for decades ceases to exist in seconds and will never be seen again nor his voice heard; as if he never existed. I knew his body was corruptible but I also believed he is more than the body. Where did his soul or spirit go?*

*Dear brothers and sisters, fifteen years ago I asked myself: how are streets of Ndegeya and Narame going to be without him? How are we going to live without his morning greetings, without his smile, without his advice let alone his financial contribution? I could not find answers at that time. Fifteen years after my father's death, I learnt a big lesson and my questions were valid. The world is not always grateful; it behaves as if nothing has changed or happened after the death of someone important like my father.*

*The world still seems indifferent to the millions of people who perish everyday in unjust wars orchestrated by the powerful for their various interests. Yet these deaths affect some individuals more than others and may handicap some lives forever. Dear friends, as we celebrate fifteen years after the death of my father I thank each one of you for your support. In a special way I would like to acknowledge the love and unwavering support of my siblings in general and of Nadina in particular. On my behalf and behalf of my siblings I would like to thank Nadina for having been where our loved father could not be. She has worked tirelessly to feed us, to pay our tuition fees, to pay for our healthcare. She has provided all that we needed. I thank my father also for still believing in us and supporting us from a distance. My father —wherever he is — should now be happy and smiling that I am a priest. I thank you."*

"My brother's speech was received by a big applause and tears from women. It was emotional and vivid. It took us back to that very moment fifteen years ago." Nadina wrote in her diary that day.

# Does God really care?

⟿⟿

"…Slowly by slowly we got accustomed to living without our father's presence. I hope and pray that our father's blood will cleanse the hearts of those who organise wars and conflicts and turn their hearts into instruments of peace. With our father's death, we became orphans of both parents at a younger age. We survived without our father's presence. Life was never going to be the same again but we had to soldier on and be strong. The speeches pronounced on the fifteenth anniversary of his death showed how all of us miss our father a lot. At least we saw him being buried unlike our mother. We know where to find him even if he is no longer glued to time and space. Every time we go to Narame, we go to visit his grave first. Myself I kneel before his grave as a sign of respect and dignity and thanksgiving for all he did and was to us. I am proud of my father and thank him for his love. I hope he accepted our renewed love for him on that anniversary. We requested that he give us his children more energy to continue the job he started many decades ago and to make our dreams come true. Besides my task of ending poverty, I have now added the major task of ending wars and conflicts on our continent…" Nadina pursued her diary on the day of the anniversary.

*"I was angry with God who called him so prematurely,"* this phrase in Mzee's speech kept coming into Nadina's mind. Like Mzee, Nadina questioned the love and mercy of God after their father's death. She lost faith and wondered whether God was still good and all powerful.

"How can a good God let our father leave us so early? How on earth did he allow such a war to our beautiful nation? If God is good then He is not all powerful for he failed to maintain our father in life or even more He failed to stop the war from taking place. If He is at the same time all good and all powerful He must be ignorant about when our father was supposed to leave this world. Why did He not wait for Mzee to come and see our father or say goodbye to him? How did God think we were going to survive without our father? Was our mother not enough for Him? Could He not have waited for us to become adults and independent before taking our father? Did he not have enough technicians *there* to accomplish different kinds of jobs that He wanted our father to accomplish? How could He be so selfish? Why does He allow orphans to suffer? Why should He allow our enemies to laugh at us and rejoice in our sorrows? Whoever and whatever He is does He really care?" These are the questions Nadina keeps asking herself. She was not surprised to hear Mzee saying he asked himself more or less the same questions.

In fact, Mzee wanted to put God on trial. Mzee was convinced that God once on trial and bombarded by the aforementioned questions was never going to be acquitted. Mzee was ready to accuse God, to ask Him similar questions and even more complicated questions. He was ready to table God's faults and corresponding punishments to a judge. He was convinced God would be convicted and stripped of all the titles He has been enjoying over centuries. Mzee thought that there was no way God could remain omnipotent, omniscience and all-good at the same time without any contradiction in those terms with the evil in the world including their father's sudden death and the imminent languishing in poverty that death seemed to entail.

But Mzee confided in Nadina on the fifteenth anniversary. They had a wonderful conversation after the celebrations:

- As I look back in these past fifteen years, I realise that I was probably harsh on God. I was too selfish. Nihilism had become part of my life. A vacuum had been created in my life and I never knew how to fill it except using my instrumental reason to philosophize and to accuse God. I lost the necessary balance between reason and faith. I failed to answer well the question: Who sinned, God or killers? Mzee explained.
- God remains good and unchangeable despite the evil that we experience in our lives. I replied with a smile on my face.
- Thank you sister. That is right.

Mzee added, amazed at how I have come to know more about God.

- These past years after my father is gone, I have witnessed God's love even in moments where one would not believe that He is listening. I have seen the generosity of the people of God and other people of good will whom I suppose get their good heart and inspiration from a Force that is external to them and that is probably supernatural –it is this force that many people call God. I would be ungrateful to ignore the hand of God working in many different ways. Mzee suggested.

- So Mzee how would you then answer the Who sinned question? I asked him.
- I believe it is not God who sinned. The question of evil is a difficult and painful reality that human beings on earth have to grapple and deal with in their daily lives. It is easy to accuse God that in his omniscience, omnipotence and goodness he should not let evil attack us. But we should never forget that God gave us the ultimate gift of freedom. As human beings —and not robots or automatons —we have the ability to choose A and not B or C. There is no way God could give us the power to choose A out B and C and at the same time taking that power away for he would be contradicting himself.
- Thank you very much Mzee for that explanation, I said.

This conversation was very inspiring for Nadina. She learnt a great deal of things thanks to Reverend Father Mzee who is now professor of political thought in Sorbonne University.

# Happy birthday dear father,
## *ad multos annos*

Nadina has come to be known as a fun of celebrating birthdays since each time any of her siblings celebrates their birthday she has to find time and gifts and join in the celebrations. On her birthday, she takes an opportunity that strikes many to give gifts to her siblings thanking them for who and what they have been throughout that year. So far she has managed to be present during the anniversaries of her brothers and sisters except Mzee who virtually does not live in the country. On the seventieth birthday anniversary of her father, Nadina decided to write him an email wishing him happy birthday, if at all they celebrate anniversaries on the other side of the river. It had never occurred to her to celebrate her parents' birthday. But today she has organised an important feast and invited some few people to join the family in celebrations.

*Dear beloved Hachris,*
*Seventy years ago, on the 19th of July you were born in the small village of Narame. Legend goes that you were a healthy kid and very cute. You were always full of life and your face was*

*characterised by smile unless you were sick which rarely happened. Kids in your neighbourhood loved you so much and always enjoyed playing with you. As a teenager you came to Kayiga capital city to become part of the Youth school with the prospects of finding a job in Kayiga. This was a school that gathered the youth from all over the country to teach them technical skills. In this school you learnt various skills that would put a lot of bread on our table and would build us a shelter of which my siblings still enjoy the comfort. If you did not come to the city you would not have met our beautiful mother and we would not have been born, at least not the way we are. How destiny escapes human intelligence! Exactly twenty years ago, you celebrated 50 years of rich life as ta fille, I celebrated 25 years and Mbanda celebrated 20 years.*

*Myself and Mzee had asked you that we celebrate your 50th birthday for it was an important event in your life and our lives. You were not exactly sure which date of that important and blessed year you were born on. You had to go to the parish in the rural area to ask them to show you your baptism card to confirm the date of your birth. The jubilee was for us an occasion to celebrate your love, your generosity, your humility and resilience after all those years you spent caring for us and looking after us and indeed a precious occasion to celebrate with Mzee who was in our midst. It was for you a moment of looking back and to be happy for what you have achieved especially having us as your loved children. Celebrating life doesn't require a lot of money as you discovered that day. That day you were shining with joy and you shared that joy with us and some friends. That was one of my happiest moments with you.*

*On behalf of the children, the last born took a speech. Hoza was very excited. She knows how much you loved us and cared for us and she reiterated that in a beautiful speech and with a shining face and a smile. Dear father, allow me once again to share with you the speech of which I kept a nice record.*

"Dear beloved father, this is not just your celebration but it is also our celebration. It is not just your joy, it is our joy. This is a celebration of a life full of love, care, generosity, humility, resilience and courage; it is a celebration of our mother, of good memory, who played a big part in your life and our lives. This is a celebration of all those who made you who you are and what you are, those who made you discover the talents that you have, but also the limits. It is a celebration of parents who gave birth to you and gave a father to us. On my behalf as the family's last born and on behalf of my siblings, I would like to thank you for the love you have shown and showered upon us. Our hearts beat with gratitude for the unwavering support throughout our lives. We are who we have become because of you and because of your loving education. You were never a brutal dad. You gently corrected us and educated us to love and serve each other and our neighbour. You worked tirelessly to put bread on table and we lacked nothing with your presence. The example you have shown us will carry us the whole of our lives. It is hard to find words to express our gratitude. We promise to aim at becoming good kids and to make you proud. We shall carry our tasks in a diligent manner as you taught us. WE will always respect you and our elders. May God's abundant blessings be upon you as you celebrate an invaluable gift of life and of children that we represent. Happy golden Jubilee. We wish you many more years full of joy and energy. We wish you good health and a prosperous life."

*You were amazed at her speech and surprised how kids grow fast into intelligent beings. Then came your turn to share your joy with us. The smile on your face said it all.*

"Dear friends, beloved children I celebrate fifty years of grace, consolation and challenges. Fifty years that many of my colleagues did not reach because of the horrible events that befell our loved nation time and again. Fifty years full of experience, sports, beautiful children and good friends. Fifty years that gifted me a wonderful family. To reiterate Hoza's words, my heart beats with gratitude to all those who have made my anniversary possible; to all those who contributed to who and what I am. My message is simple: thank you. Let us not waver in doing good, in protecting all those who are vulnerable. Let us work hard to end war and conflicts that have devastated our continent for the past decades. Let us all enjoy this celebration. Let us be happy."

*We sang happy birthday for you and wished many more years to come as though we could defy destiny and become masters of life. But nobody knows what tomorrow holds. No one could discern the hearts of destiny.*

*I always pity Mzee for missing some family events, but I was glad that he was around this time. When the party was over, Mzee bid you farewell, he had to go back to his other family, the O Dei, to prepare for his flights the next day to where he was studying and you said goodbye to him. He thought he would see you again after two years. It was in their tradition that those who go to study abroad come back every two years and he was used to seeing you once in every two years. Unfortunately, and sadly that was your face to face goodbye with Mzee. How painful that is when I think about it again. He was never going to see you again after those two years since destiny decided to take you just two months before he came back for holidays.*

*Few minutes before the ceremony ended, this beautiful woman took a speech. She did not even consult the Master of Ceremony. She did not even know that it was your birthday. She had just made a routine visit to our family. The Master of Ceremony did not interrupt her speech. Her speech was so touching that it remained engraved in my mind. Even if I were not a journalist I would still have recalled it:*

"Dear Hachris, what a coincidence for me to come on your fiftieth anniversary. To celebrate your life is to celebrate my life, the life that you rescued. My fate has been linked to yours forever. I am the only one of five children to have survived the war. All my siblings and parents were killed. Do not ask me how or why for I never have energy to tell that story. I wish I was a writer so that at least I could take my pen and put on paper my painful story and share it with everyone and let them know how the world is so cruel."

*She cried. She struggled to speak. All of us were quiet. She gathered her strength and went on:*

"Dear Hachris, for a week, you hid me in the big container where you used to keep beans. You and your wife Dativa, God bless her soul, fed me every day. None of your children knew that I was here for fear that they would innocently say it in conversation with other kids who would tell their parents and the enemy would know that I was around and would come to exterminate me. When you left home running away from the war zone, I refused to go with you for I had a feeling I wouldn't pass on road blocks set by militia without being killed. If I went, I would be killed. If I remained, I would die of hunger. I chose to remain behind to spare you any burden and trouble. I did not want you to become victims. You had already done enough for me. I thought it was better to die of hunger than from the violent guns and traditional weapons. That night, I heard the voice of soldiers saying, "all those in hiding should come out for the war is over." And then I saw the light again after fifteen days of hiding in darkness. When I went back home, the house was destroyed and I never saw any member of my family. I waited for some years. But waiting for what? For who? No one showed up and I have come to live with the reality of being alone and lonely when we were born many."

She cried again. And some of us cried with her.

"Thank you very much, Hachris, for saving my life, I will forever remain gra---te----ful." She ended.

*All of us were carefully and emotionally listening to that lady. After her speech everyone was speechless. What a way to end your fiftieth anniversary. Truly, you are a hero. Not just our hero but other people's hero. You are a saint. You are missed. It is only that we do not have enough cents to ask the Catholic Church to officially declare you a Saint. Saint Hachris pray for us and teach us courage and love to face difficult times and resilience to challenges! Teach us to be compassionate with those who suffer in one way or the other. Happy 70th birthday wherever you are. I do not know whether you celebrate anniversaries at your end. But anyhow enjoy the day to the fullest. We shall celebrate your love and heroic acts at our end this evening.*

After sending this message, Nadina went to work as usual. In the evening, up to twenty people –close friends –gathered at home to celebrate the birthday of Nadina's father which she had organised very well. She opens a bottle of Champagne and she pours a bit to give to the ancestors. It was a joyful evening and was graced by the presence of her siblings including Reverend Father Mzee.

# Still a long way to go...

⌒•⌒

Having told her father how other kids are doing, Nadina feels it is now time to talk about the last born Hoza. She was very young when their father left this world.

*Dear Father,*

*There is no doubt you have been wondering how Hoza is surviving sickness. You spent sleepless nights because of her health problems that had developed to be very serious and almost chronic. Each time she would leave school to be hospitalised. She even had to abandon school for two years due to illness. No one was really certain about what she was suffering from, including doctors. When she resumed school but still with health problems you gave her school fees for the whole year in her senior 4 as if to tell sickness that your money should not be wasted and hence she should never fall sick again. She went to school and as you know she continued to fall sick though with lesser intensity than before. Even when you passed away, she must have been sick, and I remember she was writing her exam. When Mzee saw her on the funeral day, after two years of his absence he rightly said that she had lost weight visibly.*

*You wouldn't believe it if I tell you that Hoza is no longer the same. No more illnesses. But before she became normal again she had to undergo all sorts of medical tests. Hoza did an endoscopy* and through the help of our cousin doctor met with one of the best heart specialists in our country. If you want to get a special service in this country you better have someone to connect you otherwise you can even die before receiving assistance. Just like this heart specialist, all doctors Hoza met could not detect anything wrong with her health. Doctors told her to go back and study peacefully, but she kept suffering. A miracle seems to have happened. After few months of my wondering how we were going to cope with her health bills she ceased to feel ill on her chest and stomach. After you were gone, we wondered not only how we would find school fees but also where on earth we would get money for medications and various tests and scans. Hoza has never gone to see any doctor about the heart and stomach ills anymore. It is as if once you crossed the river you begged your Leader to spare Hoza with illness and the suffering that comes with it. I never believed that she would finish school not that she wasn't intelligent but because of health problems that had become chronic. She has finished high school without much interruption and she passed very well her national exams. Only flue and tonsillitis disturb her once in a while. She is happy and has just started the university. God closes one gate by opening another, she keeps repeating to me. If all goes well my salary will be increased and I should not have much trouble paying for her tuition fees. But of course as I said earlier on, this would be after struggling to organisation Rerwa's wedding. Hoza loves studying and seems sharper than Rerwa and Mbanda and she has chosen a program of three years. I have a feeling that she will not struggle like her brother and her sister did.

The good thing is that due to health insurance introduced by the country's leadership we do not have to struggle a lot in paying healthcare. Our government did of course well to establish health insurance for people to be treated but this seems not enough for it is only for small illnesses. More often one is told by doctors at the government hospitals that they cannot deal with one's illness. One *has to go to a private hospital and there a patient cannot show them government health insurance lest they throw it back into one's hands or face as we say here. In fact, to go to some of these hospitals one needs a transfer which is hardly given. Of course I am sure you are wondering how many people die in the village that are not covered by the insurance or that have sickness that are beyond the insurance? How many people would have survived if doctors took care of those who are only ensured by the simple government health insurance with the same generosity as they do to those who bring banknotes? Capitalism seems to have entered into many people's lives and most departments. This is joking with poor people's lives.*

*After the gun shot, you suffered the same fate as you waited to be transferred from a local hospital to a provincial one. Do you remember how you heroically endured suffering in an ambulance for many hours, an ambulance that could not leave for a major hospital because there was no nurse available to accompany you? Where were the nurses? One wonders. Did the doctor at the local hospital think that the ambulance driver also took medical courses? I am sure if it were one of our leaders he would have been immediately flown abroad for treatment. I wonder how some leaders can improve our medical system when they do not have a single idea of what is going on the ground.*

*Mbanda who was with you that very night was pained to see the way you were treated and vowed that one of his children has to study medicine to help all those who are suffering and ill treated at the hospital. Being in another province, I monitored that situation through the phone. I was shocked to call you three hours later and to realise that you had not moved an inch. I always get annoyed when I remember it. Sometimes I want to agree with those who blame your death on the doctor's carelessness but I do not want to be harsh for destiny is in no one's hands.*

- *It will be okay. I told you in a low and discouraged voice over the phone.*
- *It will be up to God whether I get healed or not. You replied in a tired voice and in our local language.*

*Knowing how the ambulance took long to leave the local hospital you despaired and feared for your life but you trusted God. We are in a developing country of course where medical standards are still very poor but this should not be an excuse or a justification to neglect patients. Most of those people I interview always complain that there are so many people who die because of negligence in our hospitals and who would have survived if more care was taken. Negligence should never be tolerated as long as human life is threatened and concerned. Some doctors and nurses think they can become masters of destiny and give up on some patients they think are dying. Maybe I should have done medicine and not journalism, I wondered that time. Definitely, I do not regret the choice I made of studying journalism. I will not tire in condemning unprofessional individuals no matter which department they work for. The same problem of customer care we talked about earlier on is also characteristic of hospitals in our country. The history that our country has gone through should even teach us more how to respect human life. We can no longer afford to see and tolerate suffering of fellow human being and still keep our hands into our pockets.*

*The negligence is unfortunately rampant in many nations. This negligence goes hand in hand with corruption. For instance, the aid that is given to help in health institutions is at times pocketed by some powerful and rich people. The irony is that these powerful and rich people were meant to protect the poor and the weak. The world has become like a Darwinian jungle where the weak and poor perishes while the powerful and rich flourishes. Some people do not see any loss when a poor man dies and make* noise when a rich man dies. Can they put a price tag on human life? Are they saying that human beings are not equal? Is the value of a human in what he has or what he is? What is a human being indeed? We need to understand that human flourishing is for everyone regardless of their background or status. Preventing some people to flourish can only signify the lack of an ethic to take care of all, the abandonment of morality and hence the collapse of social life since we will have condemned human kind to irresponsibility and chaos.

However, despite some shortcomings our country has done very well in the past years in some health issues. It has reduced infant mortality and morbidity. It has achieved many good recognition internationally. Many hospitals have been built in each district. But there is still a long way to go, as you would remember when you were treated at hospital. Don suggests that even the little treatment you got you owed it to the fact that your nephew was working at the same hospital. How I pity your nephew who regretted of having started his career on a wrong foot seeing you die and yet he could not do much to help you as he had wished. He wished a miracle could save you. I suppose you understand him and he now understands after some years of medical experience that death is a destiny for all of us. When it knocks we cannot escape it even when some negligence may be involved.

One may have a lot of money like a Bill Gates or be a scientific innovator of all time like a Steve Job, or the most important man on earth like a Barack Obama, but death, destiny will swallow us when time comes, no matter how much effort doctors will put in, no matter how much money people will spend, no matter how important we are, death is going to catch up with us. Every one of us will have their own turns. Some will die in terrible circumstances while others will go peacefully. This is not justifying the unprofessionalism of some doctors. Neither is it a sign of pessimism and despair but acknowledging reality and *doing our best in as much humble and loving way as we can. Probably death should die as one artist sang if we are to escape it. Death takes kids, it takes parents, it takes old people, it takes loved ones, it does not care that children will remain orphans if it takes their parents. It ignores that it is taking the whole family in war, genocide, terrorism or in a bomb shelling or in a drone strike. It is simply cruel and wicked. It has no mercy on anyone. I wonder where it came from. There are breakthrough in science and in technology but none of them is even attempting to put an end to this cruel death. But the problem is that even if we will die we infringe death on other human beings. Who are we to infringe death on others when we fuel wars and conflicts?*

*Maybe we should not blame this death. However cruel and wicked it may be, death serves as an occasion to unite those who loved each other, it makes people fulfil the ultimate purpose of their existence, meeting God, their creator. It makes them escape for good the suffering and pain of this merciless earth. Might death not be a passage indeed to life everlasting, a necessary passage which may at times be painful. It is a bumpy, rocky, thorny way taking us back to our initial purpose, to the best good, our final end. But is there no other way of passing to the other world without making people suffer? Maybe there is but what is clear is that there is no way that as our father you could have left us and yet remained with us. That is painful enough and maybe the reality of painfulness is a necessary part of our lives.*

*Despite death that engulfs our lives, your emails, your communication with us, your continuous encouragement prove to us your children that you are the "unlosable," ever lovable. Your assistance in difficult moments that the family experiences shows that you are a living dead, you are just in a different state, interceding for us, in communion with us, in our world and yet in another world. Of course I do not understand why my faith asks me to pray for you. You, praying for myself, I can understand.*

*Coming back to Hoza's news as I conclude this email. Hoza has grown to be a responsible girl. Sometimes she is able to get part time jobs to get money for her bus fare. She tells me that she is well aware how much I have struggled and that she wants to support me. She has even promised to pay for school fees of one of my kids once she is done with school and gets a good job. I always tell her that it is my responsibility to support them the way I do.*

# A journey towards peace, unity and reconciliation

~~•~~

Hachris must be wondering about the progress in his country especially after the hatred, clashes and endless conflicts that took his life. Nadina decides to write him this evening telling him how the nation has progressed.

*Peace, unity, justice and reconciliation are still taking place. It is not an easy process as you would understand. It will take many years for people to live together with others they think have wronged them without any grudges. Undoubtedly, reconciliation takes a long time and patience to be achieved. Everyone who is affected by division has to be interested in giving his hand in reconciliation. Some people suggest that true reconciliation did not take place in our country. They claim that there is still regionalism and tribalism. People from the South and the North are always accused of having caused the two previous wars our country has suffered. As a consequence, people are still wary of each other. People avoid each other. They have never learnt to forgive each other. A number of issues still show that some people are reluctant to trust others with whom they do not share the same ethnicity or region. Recently, even religion has become a source of division.*

*Families that do not share ethnicity, region or religion may not get into conflict when it is time for their children to get married.*

*Our neighbour Nadia has found a lot of oppositions to her marriage to John –her long-time friend and fiancé. Her parents have been telling her that she should disassociate with "that boy who is not of our calibre!" She has been told many times that John's ethnic group massacred Nadia's family members and therefore she should forget about him. John is from the South and from a different ethnic group than his lovely fiancé. Recently, the family of Nadia had a heated debate about her relationship with her fiancé.*

- *How dare you have such friends, have you no feelings, no emotions? Have you got such a short memory to easily forget what they did to us? Have you got no respect for your relatives who perished? You children of nowadays, you will kill me, oh. Her mother once told her.*

- *......*

- *Nadia, my daughter, I ask you to look for a new friend who is of the same ethnic group like us. Someone who understands our problems; someone who feels like us; someone who suffered like us; someone who shares our history; someone with the same vision like us. That is someone of our calibre. There is no way someone from an ethnic group of the killers can marry my daughter, we have got nothing to do with them. Let them live their lives and us we will live ours. Her father decreed.*

- *..........*

*Although Nadia always remained quiet upon hearing her parents' remarks, she was torn up, confused and wondered what to do. She remained determined however. Nadia did not heed the call of her parents. She continued to date John for she really loved him with all her heart. It has been more than five years since both of them started dating each other.*

*Last year, on the eve of the 5ᵗʰ year anniversary of their friendship, John dressed in white asked Nadia to marry him. Nadia was dressed in a nice, short white dress which showed her curvy and attractive body. She had been asked by her fiancé to simply dress in white and had no idea of what was going to take place in that restaurant. Nadia was shocked when she saw John kneeling in front of her with a golden and shining ring. She started to shed tears of joy. John was patient enough and when Nadia calmed down, John said: "Dear Nadia, will you please marry me". Nadia without hesitation replied: "I will try". Like other girls who say yes or no she knew the challenges she had been facing. But she was very happy to hear what she has been longing to hear. Five years seemed like a century for her. On the one hand, she was very happy to receive the good news but on the other hand, she wondered how her parents will take it. She had to inform them anyway. But what was clear is that she truly loved John.*

*When Nadia's parents heard that Nadia accepted to marry John they were disappointed and threatened to miss the wedding and no longer to consider her their child if she goes on to marry him. The parents thought that threatening to disown her will make her abandon what they considered her evil ways and behaviour. There was no way Nadia could abandon her ambitions.*

*Nadia informed John of what was going on but John was never discouraged because he anticipated it looking at how their 5-year relationship has been moving. The wedding preparations went ahead as planned but Nadia was shocked to realise that it was only a business of the members from the John's side who attended preparatory meetings. From her side, very few individuals would come and those are from very far away relations. Since her father and mother are very influential people in the government they influenced closed relative to boycott all events related to the relation of Nadia and John. But Nadia hoped that on the wedding day her side will change their mind and perceptions, and come in numbers to support her after realising her commitment and love to this man. On the wedding day, her parents and other close relatives never attended the wedding. Nadia could not believe it. Nadia's husband was chocked by this behaviour of his in-laws and wondered how they were going to survive this. He started doubting a little bit about the future of their family. But he quickly dismissed the doubt. When the wedding finished the two couples were now on their own and had to see together how to move along despite the lack of support from the bride's family. They discussed the issue at length as they always did when they were faced with difficult challenges.*

- *My dearest husband, to a great extent, marriage is a personal thing. Do not worry much about the fact that my parents are not supportive of our love. Love between couples is what matters. If my parents loved you but myself did not truly love you we would not go far in our marriage. But I love you very much. She said to her husband quoting what I had told her before when she came for advice.*

- *I love you too sweetheart! But still how are we really going to live like this without having a visit and support from your family? It is like you are an outcast in your family? Love of the in-laws is also very important. But you are absolutely right that what matters the most is love between couples. John told her.*

- *No one will stop us from loving each other. No one is going to build our family. We are not going to allow anyone destroy our love or mess up with our happiness and destiny. Ethnicity or what was done by people from your ethnic group is not the reason why we should not love each other or marry each other. I am surprised at how an educated family like mine can reason like those who never went to school. Nadia retorted.*

*When Nadia got married she was a few months pregnant. This has been a trend among girls and boys who are about to get married but we will have to keep campaigning so that we despise this new culture. We should encourage our kids not to have sexual intercourse before marriage. When Nadia gave birth to her first baby boy, neither her mother nor her father came to visit her and congratulate her. She really became an outcast of her family, an enemy and a stranger in her family simply because she married someone they did not want.*

*Even up to now Nadia's family is still resisting to befriend John's family. In my conversation with Nadia I always help her question her family. How does someone generalise what has been done by some individuals to the whole family, to the whole ethnic group or to the whole region? How can people have a hard heart like that? I think there is need to intermarry like it happened in the past in our own families. We are a resilient people from the same nation and we should avoid creating boundaries and division whatsoever. We should avoid whatever can divide us and destroy the economic progress that we have thus far achieved. Our leaders should keep encouraging reconciliation among families, region and ethnic group. What unites us is more important than what could divide us.*

*Of course there are parents who do not care which ethnic group their in-laws come from. But there are others like Nadia's parents who can never tolerate that. If we are to build the nation we have to do it together. We have to forgive. We have to move towards the other who has already taken initiative and is already coming towards us. For reconciliation to take roots we have to share meanings and horizons.*

*One realises that the government still has a long way to go in instructing its citizens to coexist and to embrace reconciliation. As a journalist I meet many people who believe that there is need for the government to engage people into discourse so that they could come up together with better solutions to their problems. In this discourse, people will share their stories and become aware of the shared history, shared meanings and develop shared understandings, all of which are key to the survival and integration of any society. The top-bottom way of solving political and social issues is not always the best. Sometimes a bottom-up solution is needed. Only then do people get integrated and participate in decision making about what affects their lives. If all affected in decisions are not included some get marginalised and excluded.*

*There was a period that scared people in this country when bombs and grenades would be thrown where people get commuter buses, at the market and other places where people would be gathered. Security people have worked hard to track down those people who cause chaos among people and the judicial system has already judged and condemned some of them. We are now lucky that grenades have reduced for they had created fear and had made life in our country look short, nasty and brutish just like Hobbes described the State of Nature. Of course some of our neighbouring countries are still suffering from various woes that affect us, or that affect the common people. It is unfortunate that millions of people in different nations have died in different conflicts and thousands have become refugees, orphans and widows. It is heartbreaking to know that innocent people have died and continue suffering just because of the interests of few individuals.*

*Some countries support rebels with ammunitions and intelligence to destabilise other countries and hence get what they would not have obtained in time of peace. For example, rebels help these countries in their quest to steal minerals. Unfortunately, where elephants fight, the grass suffers. Where the powerful fight it is the weak who suffers the most. I feel for millions of people who have perished in wars and others who have suffered the loss of their loved ones. Only someone who never experienced war and the immoral person can wish to experience war.*

*Despite various problems that our nation encounters, its economy has improved very much. We are one of the fastest growing economies in on the continent. Corruption –at least the unprofessional one – has almost vanished for it is punishable seriously by the law and the office of the ombudsman is keen to publish names of all those who are involved in acts of corruption. Mother will be happy to hear that women are now part and parcel of administrative posts and thus included in decision making processes. Unlike before, there are now a huge number of women in the parliament. Of course it is one thing to be represented in the parliament as a woman by women and another thing to benefit as a woman. Many women are still living in abject poverty. But definitely women have benefited in one way or the other from these changes. I suppose in the future there will even be a big number of women whose lives will change forever. We are proud of the fact that the number of women that die while giving birth has plummeted, women have learnt to support each other in cooperatives of all kinds. Women were given chances to access education and many took the opportunity.*

*It is marvellous that people are taught that they have dignity and no one gives them this dignity apart from themselves. Our people have lost their dignity in various wars and conflicts that tore apart our beautiful nation and hence it is good to bring dignity back. It is important to work hard so that every humankind –no matter their colour, background, nation, ethnicity, region, etc – have their dignity.*

*The most successful TV emission I have conducted in my few years as a journalist was entitled: Dignity: Its Meaning and Implications. Dignity entails independence in all levels be they economic, politics, religion, etc. Our leaders always suggest that: You cannot always hold your hands to the giver waiting to be given. What if he does not give you anything? What if he gives you but attaches difficult conditionalities? Why should we keep relying on the rest of the world when we have human resources to develop our nations? Some people retort that it will be difficult for our African countries to survive without aid. Most of them have at least 30% of aid from mighty nations. The success with which we manage to live decent life without relying on foreign aid will set the tone for other countries.*

# Empowering orphan girls

～•～

As a journalist, Nadina loves talking to people to get a sense of how they feel. She always believes that the media is there to influence politicians so that they can make decisions that are just, fair, informed and impartial and that they can respond to the needs and interests of the people they govern. Having interviewed many politicians, she has come to realise that some of them are not much aware to what extent common people are suffering. They live in their ivory towers and think that everyone is more or less okay.

Some of them always have their meetings in five star hotels even when they are discussing poverty. They listen to scholars who have written good books on poverty and forget to visit the very poor people on the ground. Their meetings in the end have little, if any, impact on the common poor people at the grassroots. A number of leaders are not affected by the prices that hike most of the times nowadays with the economic crises that seem to have become the order of the day. In such cases, they may not make decisions that are in the interests of the people.

One of Nadina's recent TV programs was about "The Empowerment of Orphan Girls" when she interviewed some important personalities in the county. She has decided to share the program with her dad:

*Dear Hachris, please find attached the copy of the TV program that I conducted last week.*

*In my introduction I explained how different girls have found themselves orphans. Many are those who had their parents killed during rampant wars and conflicts in their respective countries, others are HIV and AIDS orphans and many others do not have any idea who their parents could be. I explained the consequences that come with being orphans like bad living conditions, lack of education, bad health. These orphans are not always lucky to have someone to help them achieve the dreams of their lives. Some live on their own, as heads of families, others are roaming on streets. Some people seem not to care about them or do not even know that they exist.*

*After this introduction, I introduced my guest speakers, Dr. Eric —secretary of state in the ministry of education —; Prof. Alice —minister of women emancipation — and Sr. Betty —the superior general of the Benekobwa congregation all of whom are highly involved in women emancipation, education and care of the girl child.*

*Ladies and gentleman, welcome once again to this program. Many girls in our country and in other countries are still handicapped by various problems that come with the country's and our continent's history. The three of you, I believe, have contributed a lot in making the life of the girl child better and in a special way you have helped orphan girls not to feel isolated from others but to be part of the society, a society that cares and loves them. This nation has indeed registered more progress in the area of promoting the girl child and is recommended by many donor nations to use aid quite well and for its purpose. But some people still feel that there is still a long way to go. What do you think about the empowerment of an orphan girl?*

*Dr. Eric: Mrs Nadina, there are a number of girls that have been orphaned because of the various reasons you mentioned.*

*Our country has realised that a girl child is as important as a boy child. This would have been something unheard of in the past three decades. In my ministry we even take more care when the girl is orphan and has no one to help her because we know she can fall victim of all sorts of problems like unwanted pregnancy which may even result in abortion which is punishable by the country's law or could lead to her death. For instance, the common topic is the issue of sugar daddy. This is about married men who mislead ladies by giving them a lot of money and other expensive objects, and as a result tricking them into having sex with them. These girls risk contracting different illnesses including HIV and AIDS. We have helped many orphan girls to go back to school and we will keep doing what we can to take more girls to school because we believe that education is the key to success. We want to make sure these girls are aware of the above dangers so that they may guard against easily falling for sugar daddies and anyone who can abuse them. We shall ensure that those who exploit and abuse young girls are severely punished by the law.*

*Thank you very much Dr. Eric. That is a very good intervention and I am sure there will be questions from the audience. Let us hear from Prof. Alice.*

*Prof. Alice: we collaborate with the ministry of education and pay school fees for a number of orphan girls at all levels. We want to make sure that the number of those who go to school could be increased and at the same time drop outs reduced. We hope fund donors will heed our call. In line with the Millennium Development Goals, we want all orphan girls to attend at least primary school. Slowly by slowly that target will shift to making all orphan girls attend at least secondary school and then eventually undergraduate level at college. Those who, due to the lack of intellectual aptitudes or other preferences, cannot go to formal schools we help them do some skills like tailoring, hair dressing, micro-business, etc. so that they can take care of themselves in the future. We bear in mind that a girl is the heart of the family and so more care should be taken to provide her with what she needs. Those who excel receive scholarship to universities abroad. Each year we have managed to give scholarships to twenty orphan girls. But the number is still little compared to the demands. Hopefully we will get more sponsors in the future so that we can increase the number of those who receive these types of scholarships. I would like to recommend the efforts of the government in this area and thank all those organisations that support us in giving adequate education to the girl child in general and to the orphan girl in particular.*

*Me: Prof. Alice, I am grateful for your contribution. Indeed, women are the heart of the family as our ancestors discovered. If the heart is not functional we cannot talk of the person. We therefore need to protect the heart as much as we can. It is very important that girls receive solid education so that they can also contribute in developing the nation and more importantly in being part of decision making. Let us now hear from Sr. Betty.*

*Sr. Betty: Thank you very much Mrs Nadina for having invited me on this program. My congregation is particularly interested in empowering orphan girls. We have built a number of schools across the country for that purpose. We collaborate with the ministry of education that sends us those children and the ministry of women emancipation that pays for them. We also give scholarships to some of them who excel so that they could help in the leadership of our country in the future. We are pleased that there is that collaboration. In the near future, we hope to build more schools to accommodate even more orphan girls. We can boast that some of those orphan girls we have educated are now part of decision makers in this country. We hope the good values we taught them will guide them as they represent those who elected them.*

*Me: Thank you very much Dr. Eric, Prof. Alice and Sr. Betty for your wonderful contributions. I will come back to you as time allows. We have someone on the line, let me take their phone call.*

- *Allo, yes.*
- *Hello.*
- *I'm pleased to have you on our TV station and welcome to our program. What is your name please and where are you speaking from?*
- *This is Janet calling from the Southern province. Thank you for this interesting program. I thank the three speakers for what they have said. However, I am surprised your guests are priding themselves in what they have done, when there are many of us in the Southern province who have no one to pay for us and yet we have been longing to go to school for many years. Myself, I dropped when I was in senior 5 after my mother died. I had no one to pay for me since my father passed away when I was a kid. It is five years since I was in school. How I wish I could go back again. I am saddened by the fact that I always topped the class but just because of lack of money I cannot be allowed to study. I cannot even be allowed to study and pay the fees later when I am employed. I hope our three speakers will do something for me together with other poor and orphan girls here in the Southern province as soon as they can. Thank you.*

Me: Thank you very much Janet. Dr. Eric what do you have to say about Janet's claim?

Dr. Eric: I am not sure how true that claim from Janet is. But I will investigate and see how many orphan girls are in that province and why they were not attended to when our ministry has a branch there.

Me: What Janet said is more or less the same thing I heard before when I visited a certain district. I understand money is released by your ministry to pay for these girls but the money sometimes ends up in the pockets of rich people who are in charge *of the orphan girl program since they pay for ghost students i.e students who do not exist, and yet those for whom the money was meant receive nothing. The other complaint is that this money destined for orphan girls ends up being used to pay for those who are not orphans simply because they have connections with those who work in the program. In brief, there seems to be corruption going on in this area. Don't you follow up how money was used and whether it was really used and for the right purpose? Some people say that what you are meant to believe is different from what is happening on the ground and maybe, some people say, once in a while you should be going to the grassroots yourselves to monitor the situation rather than remaining in your offices.*

*Prof. Alice: People just talk whatever they want of course and you cannot stop them from talking. What I know is that our ministry is working hard as I said before and as Dr. Eric suggested we shall find out not only what Janet said but the issues you raised as well. But so far the money has been used for its purpose. In fact, since Janet is the first to speak and has shown so much interest in the program, she is now included among those who will receive tuition fees for next academic year.*

*Me: Thank you very much dear guest speakers. Could I ask Sr. Betty to say a closing prayer as we put an end to our program? Those who have other questions can put them on our Facebook page and we shall answer them next time. You can also tweet me at @LNadina.*

*Sr. Betty: We thank you dear God for the love you love us and in a very special way the way you love every single orphan girl. We are the instruments of your love. We ask you to touch the hearts of people of good will to help us assist these innocent girls. We ask you to touch the hearts of those, if any, who embezzle the funds that are reserved for these innocent girls. We ask you to console these girls. Amen.*

# Political life

Nadina's father used to follow closely the political life of his country. He always encouraged his children when they grow up to make sure they contribute positively to the positive image of their country and that they become instruments of peace, unity and reconciliation in their country that was torn by conflicts and wars. Nadina feels it is important that she updates her father on the political situation of her country today.

*Dear father,*

*It is a common song to hear leaders suggest that a person has inalienable rights, and in fact most of these rights are engraved in the country's constitution. But it is, in many countries, another thing to put written constitutions into practice. For many years, our nation was accused of hampering human rights, freedom and dignity. Today, our country seems to have improved the way it treats its citizens and especially the opposition. But some human rights activists still believe there is still a long way to go, there are plenty of things to be done.*

*Politicians in the opposition and journalists are still mistreated. Some journalists are reported to have disappeared and organisations like Human Rights Watch and Amnesty*

*International have pointed fingers to the government since those journalists who disappeared and those who were killed were very critical of the government. Civil society organisations don't function easily they have to be sanctioned or co-opted by the government if they are to get a guarantee to do something. Of course if they are co-opted it means they will not benefit much those they are meant to serve for they will be serving the interests of the government and the powerful and the interests of those who are part of those organisations.*

*People wonder whether the notions of democracy and systems of rights seem to fail us or we are the ones failing them. They wonder whether democracy is just a white man thing which cannot work in Africa. More than fifty years of independence but still we haven't progressed very much on the road of democracy and respect of human rights. Some people believe that we need to give enough time to our continent and may be something good will come out of our continent. Unlike in your time, now we have adopted multiparty system but the role of other parties is still insignificant simply because the main party does not give them enough space to function. You never had a chance to vote for the president in your life time. Now we can. Last year I voted for the second time. But most of the times we know who is going to win. When the main party is accused of not following the principles of democracy, it responds that democracy has to be put into our country's context and adapted to our own values and culture and time.*

*Although there is still a long way to go, we seem to have made some progress compared to your time. It is this political life that has allowed economic growth especially in Kayiga city as I told you. But politicians should ensure that other parts of the country benefit from economic development as well. After all, we are not cursed but we need to take our destiny into our hands. We need to avoid the politics of division that has characterised our country and let us into wars and almost annihilated our beloved nation.*

*We need to respect the other person and always wish the best for him and try to contribute to this best. Our leaders need to ensure there is rule of law and that they abide by the constitution and other laws and promote the culture of peace.*

# Life after life

~—•—~

For the first time, Nadina has started writing in local newspapers. She has become popular on TV and her documentaries are becoming famous but she had never tried to write. Her life has been so much affected by communication with her father in the recent past that she decided to kick start her writing career with a column talking about "Life after life". Since she is still not sure whether other people have also started using the communication method she is benefitting from she did not want to talk about it yet. When one considers the amount and content of reactions to her column, Nadina seems to have touched the hearts of many.

Instead of sharing with her dad the content of her column, today she decides to have a sort of conversation with her father on why she believes in life after life.

*Why do I really believe that you, dear father and mother are somewhere enjoying life after life? Are the emails I have received from you in the recent past a guarantee that you live on after crossing the river? The little smile on my face on the day of your death is a reason to show that I believe in life after death or rather life after this life. Reason alone can never justify the other life, life after death. Reason has its own limits and the life where you are* is one way to show that reason is limited. Nihilism and secularism have taken roots in our capitalist and secular world. People seem to have lost their faith and meaning of life. They believe that life here on earth is the only kind of life there is. Once people die, that's it, they are gone for good and there will be no other life. No wonder they try to maximize happiness and enjoyment of life once they are on earth although at times this maximization leads into all sorts of evil and may turn against the person who wants to maximize.

I am convinced that just as we cannot prove life after death we cannot disprove it. But I believe that there is life after life and you, father and mother, seem to be the testimony to that. It is not just that you live on in my mind and in my person as your child and descendant but I believe your souls and spirit exist somewhere. Is it possible that I am mistaken?

Is it a coincidence that I received an answer after you answered my plea and prayer soon after your burial on various issues I had asked you especially the one of assisting me in taking care of my siblings? What about other times I run to you and you seem to intercede for me? Is it just what is hidden in the subconscious when I hear you giving me advice through dreams?

On the day you were buried people were surprised to see Mzee throw two items in your grave. They wondered in vain what he was trying to do. Was that witchcraft? One friend of mine pleaded with me to explain to her the reasons why Mzee had acted so bizarrely.

- What did your brother really drop in the grave when your father passed on? Many people seemed to look at him and to wonder what was going on in his mind. My friend told me once in a conversation.
- Do you really want to know? He dropped a pen and a wrist jewel. I replied.
- Why did he do that? She asked.

- .....
- *After a moment of silence and hesitation I answered. The pen signifies a lot of things when it comes to my father. First of all it is one of the best instruments my father liked using the whole of his life. It was always hanged on his shirt, ready to write each information that was important to him. Each time he would make a shirt sworn he would ask them to leave space where to put his pen. Even when he would buy a shirt with no place for the pen on the pocket he would take it to the tailor who had to create that space-hole for the pen. That attitude struck all of us his children in our entire life. It is the very same pen that he used in his daily activities of carpentry, water plumbing and construction. I still remember the straight lines he traced everyday in his atelier without using any ruler. For some reasons, Mzee believed that our dad would need a pen in the land where he was going. Since it is one of the best things that my father cherished and it is in many ways a simple item, Mzee decided to offer him a pen. It was a sign of recognition for the many services he has rendered to the world and to its transformation. There was no doubt that my father had changed the world and made a huge difference. Even if the pen would not be needed in the other land where my father was going, the pen will remind him of his wonderful activities and tireless work he did as he tried to eradicate poverty in his country that he loved.*
- *But who told Mzee that there are no pens where he was going or that he needed any reminder or that he needed a pen at all? My friend retorted.*
- *Mzee gave him a pen not that there are no pens over there but a sign to remind him of the kind of life he cherished here. Maybe once in a while he uses that pen I gave to him. I believe it keeps him in communication with us.*

*Dear father, do you sometimes use the pen Mzee gave you? Tell me so that I tell the sceptics. But maybe they would not believe. If they do not listen to those alive how will they believe those they think are dead anyway? I told myself as I conversed with my friend.*

- *What about the second object? My friend insisted?*
- *The wrist jewel is something that Mzee cherished a lot. He had recently purchased it on his first trip to Livingstone in Zambia. He gave it to father as a reminder of those foreign lands my father toured when he was going to play basketball.*

Nadina is convinced that writing series of email to her father will be in vain if she thought he would not listen.

"Am I making illusions to myself? Is it just the debt I owe him when he asked me perhaps jokingly to note all the difficulties we underwent as a family? But how come I receive my father's emails too? Is it someone who is playing with my mind and hacking into my emails? But how does he get the information that our father had about us before he died?" she wrote in her diary yesterday.

Nadina knows it is not easy to believe that there is life after life because human beings like empirical evidence and yet cannot get empirical evidence about the life where, let us say, her father and her mother are. But surely, having inherited fatherhood from her father to raise her siblings in so difficult conditions is a sign that she is a reincarnation of her father. But her parents do not just live in her they seem to exist somewhere although she may not know in what forms and exactly where.

Now that she has started writing, Nadina is hoping that soon she will be able to start informing others about her methods of communicating with the other world. Once others started using the same method there will be less doubt about life after this life.

# Husband of the year

—•—

*After realising how my siblings have struggled after you departed from us and how I struggled to take care of them I wondered what I can do to make the lives of other orphans better. I am lucky I have a good, loving and understanding husband otherwise it would have been hell taking care of my siblings. Many are the families that are far richer than mine but whose wives complain a lot that their husbands are stingy and cannot give any cent to their niece or nephew and cannot allow their wives to help their siblings in any simple way even if these women earned higher salaries than their husbands. They argue that what belongs to the family is for the family and should not be used to help other members of the extended family but rather to be enjoyed and used for family projects. But what one realises is that despite having many things these couples are not happy for they lack the ingredient of what makes one happy. I guess that is what you said that having is different from being just like intelligence and character are distinct although complementary.*

*I always wondered what I could do to thank those who have assisted me to help my siblings, those who have made me a good father to my siblings. I got an idea drawn from my culture and tradition: giving a cow as a sign of gratitude and thanksgiving. Recently, we decided to give two nice cows to Father Auka and*

*Father Nganga in gratitude for what they did for my two sisters. Father Auka and Father Nganga have already promised that they will come to show gratitude for the nice cows that we offered them as our tradition allows."*

I wish Father Francis of Rome was near so as to be included in the cow giving ceremony. But if I ever get a chance to go to Rome I will also look for a token of appreciation for the big and unforgettable contribution he made to my family. For the time being I have written an email to Father Francis.

"Dear Father Francis,

Greetings from Kayiga. I am Nadina –Mzee's sister –working as a journalist in my country. I have never met you but I appreciate you very much and recognize the great contribution you have made to our family. It will always be remembered and will go down in history as having allowed Rerwa, my little sister, to begin a dream that she never thought would come true of going to the university. In one year or so she will graduate from their university. In a few months' time she will get married. She has asked me to tell you that she will never forget what you and the O Dei congregation have done in her life. Dear Father Francis, may you be blessed for ever more.

*The cow that was given to Father Auka was bought by Hoza in her first salary. As soon as she graduated two months ago she was hired by a company. Having taken a 3 year program she finished before her elder sister Rerwa. The cow that was given to Father Nganga was offered by Rerwa since it was the calf that is given birth by the cow that she was offered during her traditional wedding as a dowry. This ceremony took place six months ago. In our culture, traditional wedding take place before religious wedding.*

*Surprisingly, in the same ceremony, father you will not believe, Mzee gave me a cow also which is a great-grand-calf of your cow. Since he is the one who buried you, we had given him the cow that would be produced by the cows you left behind. Finally, I gave a cow to Mzee – I was in no way imitating what he did for I had planned this act long time ago –for having never abandoned us and having given us a good friend like Father Francis. Half these cows were dedicated to you father and another half to our mother. Mbanda coloured the whole ceremony by giving a vehicle to my husband. Mbanda –in the presence of all the guests –handed the keys of a white Range Rover to my husband. He joked that this vehicle is as an award for the best husband of the year. My husband as always promised to support the family and to support me as I support other people in need.*

*During this cow giving ceremony, I did what had been on my mind for many decades. I opened a Foundation to help orphans especially those who like myself are heads of families. I know there are many orphans in our country due to terrible wars that it went through. Many are those children, though grown up now, who had to be taken care of by their siblings. Many are those who were not as lucky as we were to get a decent education even through struggle. Many are those who struggle to eat once a day. The Foundation Hachris & Dativa, in honour of you father and mother for having been good, loving, generous and kind to us, was launched. It will support orphans in various domains including education. It will carry out research and organise conferences on peace and reconciliation. It will promote economic development and good leadership in our country. The minister of family promotion was the guest of honour and laid a stone as the process of constructing offices for the foundation begins. Many generous organisations have sponsored the foundation and many more have pledged to help for they believe it is a wonderful initiative.*

*Dear father and mother, what you taught us will accompany us the rest of our lives. I am glad my siblings have vowed to follow in your footsteps and to assist me in my quest and your quest to eradicate poverty. Very soon starting from Rerwa all my siblings will be independent with families of their own to take care of. Then I will be happy and satisfied that my efforts and energy have achieved what my heart desired when I was crying beside your tomb stone —to be able take care of my siblings.*

# Time for holidays

—•—

We may never know with certainty what goes on the other side of the river where we believe Nadina's father and mother are together with multiple other people. But Nadina has experienced direct communication with the other world of the living dead. These living dead have an influence on us to a certain extent. Having access to their Leader, they can influence him in decision making. They can appeal to pity and make their requests answered as it is the case in Nadina's father when he intercedes on behalf of his children. Happy are therefore those who have those who love them the other side of the river because they will always intercede for them.

Nadina is aware that she should never rely on the help that comes from the other side of the river and forget that individual efforts are highly required. To transform the world, she has to do her best to make the world a better place for all those who are struggling. This achievement will give her a place in the Leader's place and she will be able to influence his decisions on those loved ones who will have remained behind after one crosses over to the other side. The way people live here on earth matters a lot and impacts on how they shall be treated as far as their loved ones on earth are concerned.

- It is now time for holiday in a place where there is no Internet connection. I hope I will survive a life of not communicating with my father who is across the river. Let me send him the last email before I go on holiday., Nadina murmurs to herself.

*Dear father, I can never find ways to thank you for what you have done for us, for the good words of encouragement colouring your emails. Kind regards to our generous and loving mother. It is that time of the year where my husband, our kids and I go somewhere quiet to rest and ponder on the blessings we have received throughout the year and to recharge our batteries.*

*You will always be on my mind and in my heart. You taught us how to become women and men that our nation is proud of having. Bye for now. Peace & Love.*

*Yours sincerely,*
*Nadina.*

Just as Nadina's finishes sending the email she starts getting ready for the holiday since it is almost time that they agreed with her husband. As she is about to jump into the shower the phone rings. She thinks that it is the husband but she realises that it is a number that is not familiar to her. At first she wants to ignore it. But she decides to pick it up.

- Allo. Who am I speaking to please?
- Allo Nadina. This is the Prime Minister speaking.
- Prime Minister. You are kidding me.
- Yes it is true it is the Prime Minister of the Republic. Could you please come quickly to the office?
- ….
- Allo. Should I send my men to pick you up?

Nadina realises that it is getting serious and that she may indeed be speaking to the Prime Minister of the country. She starts wondering what she has done; whether she has committed any crime. She remembers that two weeks ago some men in uniform came to her office and her house and searched them; took her laptop for one day and returned it. Yet they did not say anything at all. She thought it was in connection of her being vocal and criticizing the government as a journalist. Nadina wondered whether she should tell the Prime Minister that she is about to go on holiday and so has no time but she decides to answer positively.

- I am sorry if I have been rude. Let me get ready and rush to the office his excellency.
- Ok. You are welcome. No Problem.

Nadina calls the husband that she has just received an urgent call from the office of the Prime Minister and that she may be late for going to holiday. The husband thought it was a joke. Some minutes later Nadine arrives at the Prime Minister's office.

- Hello Nadina. How are you? How is your job going?
- Hello Prime Minister. I am fine thank you. When you called me I was getting ready to go on holiday with my family.
- It is a well timed holiday indeed. There is too much work waiting for you once you are back. Make sure you rest well. And congratulations you have been appointed minister of information.
- Nadina was speechless, she thought she was dreaming…
- Her excellency minister, enjoy your holiday.

The Prime Minister hands her an appointment letter which she receives with trembling hands and still she cannot utter a word. She remembers that she has never had any ambition of becoming a politician. She wonders whether this would allow her to pursue her dream of fighting poverty and bringing about economic growth to her country. She almost wanted to refuse. But she remembers that she has been criticizing the government and maybe it is easy to criticise when you are not the one who does it. Now that she has accomplished her task of being father to her siblings who have already grown and that she has just launched a Hachris & Dativa Foundation, she thinks it is time for a new challenge.

- Thank you very much for believing in me. Thank you for trusting that I can contribute more to my beloved nation. ...So help me God.
- All the best indeed Minister.

Printed in the United States
By Bookmasters